# REVIVE

*The Sheysu's Gold Series Part One.*

By Sunita Venchard

REVIVE
©2014 Sunita Venchard. All rights reserved.
First edition printed 2014.

www.sunitavenchard.com

Cover design: Nino Khan, ninokhan.deviantart.com
Editing and Interior design: Amy Eye, The Eyes for Editing
Background stock images used on cover: wyldraven.deviantart.com

Sunita Venchard asserts her moral right to be identified as the author of this book.

This is a work of fiction. Names, characters, places and events are either drawn from the author's imagination or are used fictitiously and are not to be construed as real. Any resemblance to events or actual persons, living or dead is entirely coincidental.

No part of this publication may be reproduced, stored, transmitted or used in any manner whatsoever without the prior written permission of the author. For information regarding permission, contact details can be found at www.sunitavenchard.com

ISBN-13: 978-1502786944
ISBN-10: 150278694X

# DEDICATION

For Rama and Sasha
thank you for supporting and believing in me.

# THE TRAVELLERS

Sheysu clung to the uneven rocks as she made her way up the hillside. She was not aware of the blood slowly oozing from the many cuts in her hands. Cuts made by the jagged rocks she pulled herself up with. She had been travelling for two days now with little sleep, yet her body did not ache. Sheysu looked ahead but did not see, so deep were her thoughts. Thoughts of those she had left behind, those who could do nothing but wait patiently and hope for her return. Her eyes filled and the tears ran slowly down her cheeks.

The sound of horses' hooves and the clinking of carts broke Sheysu out of her tearful reverie. She looked across the hillside at the small group of travellers who were coming in her direction fast. Three carts travelled in a straight line, each identical with items hanging in exactly the same place. Even the people looked remarkably similar. Impressive horses pulled along the sophisticated carts, although they appeared designed to travel without horsepower if necessary. The tracks they left were incredibly straight. Everything about them had a structure and order.

Sheysu wiped the tears from her face, unaware of the streaks of blood left behind.

"Hellooo!" she shouted.

The travellers in the first cart waved at her. She could see them more clearly now. There were eight travellers in all, two couples and a family of four. As they got closer, their expressions became worried. Sheysu's body tensed and she stepped back, suddenly afraid. The man in the first cart jumped down and walked towards her.

"Are you alright?" he asked. "Have you been injured? Do you need help?"

Sheysu was about to say no, but then looked down at herself, saw her bloodied hands and breathed a sigh of relief, knowing now the reason for their worried looks. She now felt the many cuts on her hands, each stinging separately.

"Hold on," said the man, then shouted back to the woman on his cart. "Bring the Calendula!" The woman opened a large bag and fished out a bottle of brown liquid. She jumped down, bringing another bag with her.

When she reached Sheysu, she said, "Let me treat your wounds."

Sheysu nodded. "Thank you." Grateful for anything that would help her hands to heal.

She got some cloth and a canteen of water out of her bag and very gently cleansed Sheysu's hands. Her hands tensed with pain. The woman mixed a few drops of the Calendula liquid with some more water and then bathed Sheysu's hands with the solution. At first, the mixture stung a bit, but gradually the pain eased and Sheysu relaxed. The smell and the sensations took Sheysu back to when her mother had similarly treated her for the many cuts and scrapes she had suffered as a result of her childhood escapades. Sheysu blinked away the tears threatening to form again. The woman smoothed back the wavy tendrils of dark hair spilling over Sheysu's face and then carefully wiped it clean, revealing the olive complexion beneath. Sheysu hadn't realised there was blood there too and smiled gratefully. She must have looked quite scary.

"Where are you headed?" asked Sheysu.

"As far from here as possible," replied the man

"Why? What has happened?"

"We are fleeing our homeland, the kingdom of Mineralia."

The man lowered his gaze to the ground, hesitating. When he looked back up, it was with sad eyes. "We were once a proud people. That was before our latest sovereign, Queen Platina, began her rule of oppression. If I tell you her history, then you might be able to understand what she has done to our beloved Mineralia"

Sheysu's eyes widened at the mention of Queen Platina and she listened carefully as the man continued. "Queen Platina is arrogant and proud. She was born to a lowly family, but from the beginning, she looked down upon them, claiming she had somehow been placed with them by mistake. As a teenager her stunning looks attracted attention wherever she went. Eventually, she caught the eye of the young prince, who became besotted with her aloof but flamboyant charms. They quickly married and he was soon crowned king."

Sheysu interrupted, looking confused. "What happened to the prince's parents, the king and queen?"

"Well no one knows how it happened, but the king and queen died in a freak fire at the palace shortly after their son was married. Once the new king and queen were crowned, gossip about them filled the land. They had a stormy marriage, full of passion and blazing rows. Everyone waited for them to have children, to produce an heir to the throne. But it was no real surprise to anyone that *she*," the man's voice filled with anger, "bore no children. Her intolerance to them, which verged on hatred, was clear for all to see. The prince was a good king, and life in Mineralia continued to thrive. But then two years, to the day, after they were married, everything changed."

He took a deep breath, shuddering as he released it, his expression pained. "The king died suddenly under bizarre circumstances. Whilst shaving one day, he accidentally slipped and cut his own throat."

Sheysu gasped in horror. "How could that happen?"

He sighed sadly as if all hope had been lost. "It remains a mystery. There was much talk of foul play at the palace after his death, especially when the queen was seen stifling her laughter at his funeral. However, no one would dare to cross her. Her reputation for her wrath and ruthlessness was known by all in the kingdom. She had even banished her own family soon after her marriage. Conditions in Mineralia deteriorated rapidly. Where previously there had been a supportive, nurturing community that had provided order and structure, there is now oppression and a life of servitude to the palace. Now, maybe you can understand why we have left."

Sheysu listened to the story, her stomach wrapping itself in knots. Mineralia was where she was headed and Queen Platina was her destination. She had heard stories of Queen Platina before, but none had painted a picture quite so bleak. Gulping back her fear, she strengthened her resolve. Nothing would deter her from her mission—she had no choice.

"Where are you headed?" The man's eyes drifted over her worn clothes and scanty supplies.

"I'm…" Sheysu hesitated, knowing they would try to direct her away from Mineralia. "Going to visit relatives in the jungle just on the outskirts of Mineralia." She spoke quickly, anxious for her lie to be over.

"Watch yourself. Don't get too close to Mineralia. Queen Platina has eyes everywhere. Now, are you sure you'll be okay? You don't look like you have enough food or water to keep you going. We'd be happy to share ours with you."

"No, I'll be fine, honestly. But thank you." Sheysu breathed a sigh of relief.

"Well then, we'll be on our way." The man nodded at Sheysu before he and the woman turned and walked back towards the carts. Sheysu watched as they sped off, a cloud of dust swirling behind them.

A cold blast of wind lifted her hair and sent chills racing through her. She pulled her shawl over her head, wrapping it tightly around her shoulders and looked at the lowering sun. She needed to find somewhere safe for the night. In the distance she saw a large rock formation, which looked as if it might provide some protection from the elements. Hastily, she made her way towards it.

Sheysu found a large rock shaped like a grasping hand. She sat within its hold, sheltered from the elements by its large, stony fingers. Her stomach rumbled loudly and whilst she knew she should eat, all she wanted to do was sit and think. Think about the last few weeks and the events that had changed her life forever.

# WHY?

Every traumatic detail was etched clearly in her mind. Today was Friday. Two weeks ago, her life had been fairly uncomplicated and happy. There had been no indication of what was about to come. Last Monday her twin sister, Kora, complained of feeling ill after working hard for days on a painting no one had been allowed to see. That evening she became very hot and her fever developed quickly. Soon, her skin was burning and covered in perspiration. As the night progressed, her condition worsened, and the physician was called. He gave her many medicines, but nothing made any difference. The next morning, she slipped into a coma and her fever lessened. Her condition seemed to stabilise but she remained in a coma. The physician said there was nothing more he could do and that it was now a waiting game to see what nature would decide.

Sheysu's mother, Euphorbia, stayed by Kora's bedside as if tied to it. She talked constantly to Kora, telling her stories of their childhood, and how special they were. The stories she told differed greatly from Sheysu's own memories of growing up. They lived in the kingdom of Planta and she had always felt she and her sister were outsiders. They had always been different to everyone else around them and the fact they were twins did not help. Everything about them was unusual—the way they walked, the way they talked, and even the way they dressed. At school, they had found it difficult to make friends and their appearance was often teased. However, when they were at home, they were completely loved. Their mother and father showered affection upon them, almost too much at times.

A week earlier Sheysu had overheard her mother's two sisters talking. What she heard stopped her heart and froze it in her chest. Their words shocked her to her very core, whilst suddenly making sense of her world. Sheysu ran back to tell Kora, who was completely stunned by the news. They confronted their parents with their newfound knowledge. Sheysu remembered the look of resignation on her parents' faces; the look that said they had always known this day would come. Her mother then told them the story of how she had found a woman in the forest while collecting firewood. She recounted the story as if it had happened yesterday.

*"The woman was bleeding so heavily and cried with pain as she pushed her two baby girls, wrapped in a blanket, towards me. She pulled me close and begged me to take care of her girls. Tears were streaming down her face. She said she had no one else to look after them. I tried to stem the flow of blood, but to no avail. The woman was dying. I had only just got married and looked at the two little girls knowing I could not in my heart refuse to take them in. How could I say no? My hands were*

*tied. I promised her I would take care of them. The woman relaxed and asked to hold her babies. I placed them in her arms and she snuggled her face close to theirs and whispered to them. The tiny girls wrapped their arms around their mother's head and with that, she sighed her last breath. She was gone. She was your mother and the babies were you and your sister. I brought you both home where you were instantly accepted by your father. We have always loved you as our own, and as the years went by, nature decided you were to be our only children."*

The bang of the door and her father's entrance had startled Sheysu from her thoughts. Her mother was still sitting by the bed, but no longer talking. Instead, she held a handkerchief in her hands which she continuously wrung, tying it up and then untying it, as if the action gave her some relief from the situation.

Their father, Geran, had been all over town and the next villages to see if he could find someone who could help his beloved Kora. He had not slept and would not stop until he found the help he needed. He was told by many to visit Camphora, who was known for her prophetic dreams. She, they said, would hold the key to her cure.

The next day Sheysu and her father travelled half a day to the village where Camphora lived. On the way Geran told Sheysu how Camphora had developed the ability to see into the future. Camphora was only eighteen, the same age as Sheysu. Ten years earlier she had been struck down with cholera. The local physician tried in vain to cure her, but none of his medicines had any lasting effect. Eventually, he resorted to using the plants he remembered from his youth. He took sap from a nearby conifer tree his mother had used when cholera had struck their family. He remembered how she had mixed it with alcohol and water, and then diluted it further, as it was too toxic to use in its crude form. He then tried this mixture on Camphora, who responded almost immediately. Over the next few days, she regained her strength and made an almost full recovery. However, the illness left a strange effect in its wake. She began to have the most vivid dreams accompanied by some of the symptoms she had experienced whilst ill with cholera. She told her family about the dreams, which could come at any time and seemed so real, often involving people she knew. One by one the events in her dreams came true. Over time she learnt to control when she had the dreams, and even the people who featured in them, as if she were creating her own world. People came from far and wide to hear her prophecies. One thing they soon realised was that the prophecies were not set in stone and could be changed if acted upon. The changes, however, were not always beneficial.

Camphora was sitting outside. Her red hair contrasted sharply with her pale, white skin. Her face was tinged with blue as if from coldness. She sat next to a large fire, wrapped up tightly with a thick fur blanket. Camphora smiled and nodded at Sheysu and her father, acknowledging she knew why they had come. She closed her eyes and, within seconds, appeared to be asleep. The fire crackled loudly, snapping the silence, its flickering flames reflecting on her face, dancing and darting across it. Her eyes moved rapidly under her eyelids, and then suddenly, she threw off her blanket and her face contorted in painful spasms. Her lips curled upwards, baring her teeth and saliva began frothing at the corners of her mouth. She opened her eyes, her expression wild, her pupils dilated and pointed at Sheysu.

"You are dying!"

Sheysu was taken aback and quickly replied, "No it's not me. It's my sister. We look the same."

"No, you too are dying! The bond between you and your sister is strong, strong enough for the sickness to travel through it."

Sheysu felt her legs go weak. Suddenly, the earth beneath her felt soft. She could feel herself sinking into it. Her head was full of electricity, messages firing around but nothing making sense. She wanted to run, run far away, but her feet were being sucked into the ground. Her father, sensing her imminent fall, put his arm around her waist and pulled her close, holding her up. His face became more ashen, if that were possible.

"No, no," Sheysu whispered, as if saying it would make it go away.

"Yes, I'm afraid it's true." Camphora sighed.

"But how? When?"

"Your sister is weak, but she is surviving on your strength. She has, at the most, four weeks to live. You will soon begin to feel some of her symptoms. If a cure cannot be found in those four weeks, you will both die! In my dream, I saw you leave to travel across strange lands. You were looking for the mystical healer Similia. He is your only hope of survival. Go to Mineralia and see Queen Platina. She will help you find Similia. That is all the dream has shown me."

Sheysu looked at her father, her eyes wide with fear. Her body trembled and her warm, olive skin became grey as she felt the blood rush out of her.

Geran hugged her close. "Don't worry. We will find Similia together. I won't let anything happen to you and your sister. You are my life."

"NO!" shouted Camphora.

Sheysu and her father looked up, startled.

"She must go alone. In the dream she begins the journey by herself. To change the dream could change everything and spoil her chance of success."

Sheysu sobbed hysterically. She had never even been to the next town on her own. She went everywhere with her family. How would she cope travelling across strange lands? Panic coursed through her veins; her body shook violently and her breathing became so fast she felt as if she would pass out. Her sister's face flashed before her. She remembered why they had come to see Camphora, and in that second, she knew she had to do it. She had to find Similia for her sister. Camphora's words echoed in her ears. *"She is surviving on your strength."* She had to keep strong. Her sister's life and hers depended on it.

# MINERALIA

Sheysu woke up, still embraced by the stony hand. She shivered and took the shawl she had been lying on and wrapped it around her shoulders. Her stomach rumbled violently, and knowing she had to keep strong, she opened her brown leather bag and reached for the bread and cheese wrapped in paper. It tasted good and she wolfed down a substantial amount in seconds. She looked around at her unfamiliar surroundings, unsure of which direction to take next. From her bag she retrieved a tied roll of waxed paper and carefully spread it out on a rock, revealing the map her father had drawn before she left. It showed the directions to Mineralia. She pulled a compass from the side pocket of her bag and held it against the map which she then turned to match the compass, so they were both facing North. The map showed Mineralia being sheltered by a network of hills with a seemingly never-ending jungle to one side—the kingdom of Animalia. Looking ahead, she could see those hills in front of her. Another half a day and she would be able to see Mineralia.

Sheysu set off towards her destination, almost running, and reached the steep slopes in good time. Gazing upwards, she wondered if she had the energy to reach the top. Scouring the landscape in all directions, she sighed as there was no other way through. She began the long climb. With each step she imagined she was closer to finding Similia and a cure for her sister. It kept her tears at bay and gave her the strength to go on.

When she reached the top, she surveyed the valley below. The kingdom of Mineralia spread out before her. She looked in awe at the turrets of silver, gold, and other precious metals glittering in the sun. At the heart of the kingdom, the town of Periodica looked out of place amongst its natural surroundings. It resembled a grid with streets crisscrossing below her. She had never before seen anything so perfect, so ordered and structured. It reminded her of the travellers she had encountered. She could imagine them living there. The streets looked as if they had been drawn with giant rulers, each perfectly aligned with the next. All the houses appeared almost identical, made with the same precision. Built on top of a man-made peak above the houses was the palace, clear for all to see. It, too, was built meticulously.

A mixture of hope and panic spread through her. This was it! She took a deep breath and ran down towards Periodica. As she walked through the streets, she was oblivious to the stares of others. She didn't notice how the ground had changed to a perfectly smooth, level surface, how every house she passed was exactly the same number of steps from the last, or how everything around her was so advanced. She looked out of place, but again, she didn't notice. Her eyes were fixed firmly on the palace and she hurried towards it.

Sheysu climbed the steps up to the palace. The silence was eerie. She had expected guards to stop her, yet there was no one in sight. Walking through the palace gates, she spotted a figure running hurriedly across the courtyard.

"Wait!" Sheysu shouted. "Please help me."

The figure stopped and motioned quickly towards Sheysu, shouting, "I am in a hurry. What do you want?"

"My name is Sheysu. I need to see the queen. My sister's very sick and I've heard the queen knows where to find the great healer, Similia."

As Sheysu got closer, she saw he was a silver-haired man in his fifties or thereabouts. His face looked sunken, with his darkly-tanned skin drawn tightly over the bones. He had a nervous air about him and his lips trembled as he spoke.

"I am Argentum Nitor, the queen's advisor. Don't you know what's happened?" he asked, looking irritated. "The queen has gone missing. Everyone in the palace is out looking for her. I'm just on my way to help the search."

"I'm coming with you," said Sheysu, now even more desperate to find Queen Platina.

"She's gone missing a couple of times before," explained Argentum as they started walking. "She talks constantly about being all alone in the world, and has to act this out before she comes to her senses. We usually find her nearby."

The queen's disappearances made Argentum very nervous. He was always very anxious to find her, since any permanent disappearance would mean massive upheaval in the kingdom and more responsibility for him. Argentum was the queen's number two. Responsibility did not sit well with him. He was very cheerful but had a nervous disposition, and his anxiety was evident in every duty expected of him. He hated being late, so much so that he was often seen loitering around public events hours before they were due to start. Appearances in public were the worst—he was seen to spend his day running backwards and forwards to the toilet. However, for all his anxiety, he was a great public speaker and spokesman for the palace, and for this, the queen valued him immensely.

Sheysu and Argentum eventually found the queen sitting in the base of a very old, gnarled tree. Argentum had remembered the queen asking about the tree a few days earlier. He exhaled loudly in relief, his body visibly relaxing as he caught sight of the queen. The queen looked up, as if it were the most normal thing for her to be sitting there, completely oblivious to the chaos and panic she had caused by her disappearance.

She looked curiously at Sheysu and said, "Who is she?"

"My queen," said Argentum, "this is Sheysu, a traveller looking for healing for her sick sister. She has heard you may be able to help."

"What makes you think I can do anything?" asked the queen.

"Your highness, I have heard that you know the whereabouts of the magical healer Similia."

"Ah, the great healer Similia Similibus Curantur. Yes, I have been looking for him for some time, but he never stays in one place. It has been said that finding Similia is like peeling an onion. Each new layer reveals its own mystery to unravel. All I can give you is some ideas of how and where to find him, but the rest you must do yourself."

"Thank you, your highness. Your help is more than I could hope for."

"Yes, I am sure it is. Follow me to the palace," said the queen.

The queen was led to a nearby carriage, whilst Argentum and Sheysu followed on foot.

Queen Platina exhibited none of the haughtiness and disdain for which she was famous. She was actually being very helpful and Sheysu could not understand why.

"Is the queen usually this helpful?" asked Sheysu.

"She can be like that sometimes," replied Argentum. "However, she can change in an instant, so I warn you, get all that you need while you can, as there is no telling how long this good mood will last."

At the palace, Sheysu was taken to an elegant room overlooking the palace gardens and told to wait until the queen was ready to receive her. She was given no indication of time and paced the room anxiously. Could she trust this haughty, erratic ruler? After hearing the travellers' damning accounts of her, she feared not. Why would the queen choose to help her?

A stranger with nothing to offer in return. Something was wrong. Her instincts screamed for her to run but Sheysu blocked them out, knowing she had no choice but to stay and face whatever lay ahead.

# QUEEN PLATINA

Back in her chambers, the queen thought about Sheysu and her request. She had noticed Sheysu appeared small in stature; in fact, she had noticed for some time that everyone around her was very small. It was a strange phenomenon, but one that pleased her since she could look down on them all.

Sheysu's arrival had come at an opportune time for the queen. The queen was sick. Recently, she had been feeling constricted in her arms and legs, a sensation that grew worse every day. She feared she was dying, but could not let anyone in the kingdom know. She could not even trust her own personal physician. So far, she had made two unsuccessful expeditions for Similia, knowing her sickness was getting worse. The trips had been made under the pretence he would be a valuable asset to the kingdom. She had also sent her own trackers on numerous occasions, again without success. Time was of the essence now, as many of her subjects had begun to notice her erratic behaviour and health. She heard them whispering while walking through the corridors of the palace. There were many under her rule who would gladly see her dead or usurp her. She could not risk going on any more expeditions for fear of raising suspicion and weakening her health even further.

Sheysu could be just the one to help her. Her motivation for finding Similia was strong, and since she was not from Mineralia, no one need know what was happening. The queen sensed Sheysu would somehow find Similia. She would send Aurum to help Sheysu. He was her number one. Aurum was young but possessed the intellect of someone much older and was also a great soldier. He had been groomed as a leader from very young and was trained extensively in the art of combat.

Aurum had fought in the Great War with the kingdom of Animalia at the age of fourteen, surviving it with barely a scratch. As the king's young nephew, he had always been the natural choice to take over the throne when the king died. Aurum's mother, the king's sister, however, was weak and timid and Queen Platina had easily persuaded her and the elders that he was too young and would benefit from being under her guidance. Aurum had been ready to be king and had not taken kindly to being her advisor, but had accepted it for his mother's sake. Recently, however, he had talked about being ready to assume his rightful place on the throne. He was becoming difficult, so now was the time to remove him from the kingdom temporarily, or even permanently. A plan began to form. She would ask Mercurius to follow them. Mercurius was an anarchist, a revolutionary who answered to no one. His hatred of the king had led him to form an alliance of sorts with the queen. He was a great assassin and had helped the queen in many a sticky situation. Once Sheysu and Aurum had found Similia, Mercurius would kill them and bring Similia back to her. That would take care of her two biggest problems: her health and Aurum's right to be king.

# AURUM

Sheysu was summoned to the queen's chambers. The room she entered had a floor-to-ceiling curved glass window spanning its entire length. The views over Periodica were breathtaking. All around her, everything, even the floor, glittered and shone with a mix of many different precious metals and minerals. Argentum was standing next to the queen, moving around anxiously. The queen was seated on a large, opulent chair next to the window. Sunlight poured over her and Sheysu could see how striking she was. The queen's dark black hair, pulled back severely from her face in an elaborate design, contrasted starkly with her pale skin. Her lips, painted a deep red, did nothing to warm the coldness of her features. Her beauty was a harsh angular one with no softness to ease her haughty expression.

"Sheysu," said the queen, "your story has moved me, and so I have decided to help you. I will see that you have sufficient supplies and will send my most trusted advisor, Aurum, to help you."

"Thank you, your highness," said Sheysu, almost lost for words at her kindness.

"If I may interject, my queen," said Argentum

looking extremely worried, "who will take over Aurum's duties in his absence?"

"Why, you of course," replied Queen Platina.

"I have far too many engagements and responsibilities already, my queen."

"Well then, you'll just have to work that much harder," said the queen, visibly enjoying seeing Argentum squirm.

Argentum nodded, the colour draining from his face. "Excuse me, my queen. I need to get some fresh air." Argentum quickly left the room, looking as if he were having a hard time breathing.

Sheysu heard footsteps behind her and looked round. A young man entered the room. His jaw-length, wavy hair glinted gold in the sunlight, and his eyes, a deep turquoise blue, surveyed the room. He stopped mid-step as he caught sight of Sheysu. His piercing eyes looked straight at her. She turned away from his gaze, blushing when she realised she had been staring at him with her mouth open. He was strikingly beautiful. His face was smooth and taut and his tanned skin stood out against his white tunic shirt. His smooth, muscular chest was visible in the opening of the tunic, over which he wore a leather waistcoat. Around his neck he wore a small golden amulet suspended by a thin leather strap.

"Ah, Aurum," said the queen, "you have decided to grace us with your presence."

Sheysu was taken aback; Aurum was young, much younger than she would have imagined a queen's advisor to be. He barely looked twenty-five.

"Aurum, this is Sheysu. She will tell you why she has come for my help."

Sheysu proceeded nervously, telling Aurum about her quest, unable to meet his gaze. She omitted the part about her own imminent death, fearing they would think her incapable of travelling.

The queen looked at Aurum. "I have a special mission for you. You must do all you can to help Sheysu find Similia. Her story has moved me greatly and I have promised to do all I can in my power to help her. You will go with her and help her succeed."

"Queen Platina," said Aurum, looking irritated, "surely you don't need me to go on this journey. I can send the Chief of Guard, Ferrume. He is a good man, a great soldier and tracker. I think my services are best utilised here in Mineralia."

"Aurum, as I have said, I will do all that is in my power to help this young lady and that includes sending my very best, which is you. Now I will hear no more on the matter. You will leave first thing in the morning."

"As you wish, my queen." Aurum sighed heavily on the last words.

Sheysu listened to the exchange, feeling unjustifiably annoyed that Aurum did not want to help her. Did he think her problem was insignificant? Her face became hot as she felt the anger well up in her. He looked at her, his expression one of frustration. If he didn't want to help her, then she didn't need him, especially if he was coming against his will.

"Queen Platina," Sheysu said firmly, "I will be

fine on my own. Just tell me how to find Similia and I'll be on my way."

"Nonsense," retorted the queen, "you won't survive on your own. Aurum is the best chance you have of finding Similia and saving your sister. He has travelled extensively, often in dangerous and war-torn circumstances. You could do a lot worse than have him as your companion. You will leave in the morning. Your supplies will be ready by then. Tonight, I will piece together the information I have on Similia. I have instructed the servants to lay out fresh clothes for your journey. You may go and rest before the journey ahead."

Sheysu looked up and nodded awkwardly, unaccustomed to such generosity. There was no point in upsetting the queen with her request to go on her own. She would go with Aurum if that's what the queen wanted, but she would just have to keep focussed on the task ahead instead of her annoyance at him. Before the queen could change her mind, Sheysu started walking towards the door, keeping her head down.

"If that is all, my queen," said Aurum, "I will excuse myself so I can begin preparations for the journey."

"Yes, Aurum, that is all."

There was a brief, uncomfortable moment as Aurum walked beside Sheysu to the door, but she breathed a sigh of relief as he nodded at her and went in the opposite direction. She walked back slowly through the unfamiliar corridors. Servants shuffled past her, their heads bowed, not a sound except for their muffled footsteps. She could almost feel the weight of fear that kept their heads lowered. The walls were lined with paintings of the queen, each with a different pose, yet all with the same mocking smile. She stopped to look at one more closely. The queen's dark eyes stared back at her, cold and merciless. A sense of doom fell upon her. How would she ever succeed in her quest with her only help coming from the questionable Queen Platina and the reluctant Aurum?

# AND SO THE JOURNEY BEGINS....

Sheysu slept amazingly well and woke feeling refreshed. She hadn't realised how tired she was. The bed was so comfortable, more luxurious than anything she had ever experienced. Stretching out, she gazed at the glittering ceiling above—a kaleidoscope of precious metals. For a few seconds, she had not a care in the world, only that half-awake, blissful ignorance before the troubles of the world are remembered. She looked across the room at her bag lying on a chair, her father's map poking out of the opening. Waves of guilt washed over her. How could she enjoy such a sumptuous sleep while her sister was in a coma dying, and her mother and father were anxiously waiting? Leaping out of bed with a newfound urgency to resume her quest, she was about to put on her torn, grubby top and skirt when she noticed the new outfit hanging on the door.

The clothes were unfamiliar, having never worn trousers or boots before, but they seemed more practical than her skirt for the journey ahead. The trousers were like nothing she had ever seen—made from material that felt smooth but tough at the same time. She pulled them on and they stretched magically with her body as she fastened them. A leather belt with pockets, for what purpose she did not know, didn't fit around her waist, but felt right when she slung it around her hips. She pulled on the brown boots that felt like leather, but the smell was entirely different, almost metallic. They were a perfect fit. Next, she slipped the white, sleeveless top over her head. It was pleasantly cool to the touch. Finally, she put on the short, brown jacket which was incredibly warm for a garment so light and thin.

There was a knock at the door and a muffled voice said, "The queen requests your presence in her chambers."

"Thank you!" she shouted through the door. Sheysu pulled her fingers through her wavy hair, trying to bring some order to it. As she was leaving, she glanced briefly in the mirror to check her hair, only to stop for longer when she caught sight of herself in her new clothes. She almost didn't recognise herself. The figure-hugging trousers and jacket showed off all her curves. She had never thought of trousers as being particularly feminine, but these were altogether different. She liked what she saw, and with a half-smile, she left the room.

Aurum was already with the queen when Sheysu entered. Again, he stared intently at her as she walked in and Sheysu bristled with anger as she remembered his reluctance to help her.

"Ah, I see you slept well," said the queen. "You look rested. Good, you can start your journey with renewed vigour. I have been trying to piece together information on how to find Similia from my previous expeditions. We were unlucky, but a few times we came very close. I think it is essential that those looking for him are either sick themselves or have a strong connection with someone sick. For that reason, Sheysu, I think you have an excellent chance of finding him. There has never been a detailed description of Similia. Some doubt his existence, whilst others say he changes form as he moves through the different kingdoms, sometimes human, sometimes not. Everyone who claims to have met him describes him differently. I have been in touch with my guards and trackers. They have reported the most recent encounter with Similia was in the kingdom of Animalia. I suggest this is where you start. To find Similia you must open your minds and let your intuition and senses take over. You may believe that rational thinking and logic can help, but they can also cloud your instincts and stop you from making the obvious choice. Keep your mind free, something I have never quite mastered, and trust in yourself, and then Similia will come to you. Your supplies are ready and waiting, so run along. You have no time to lose."

The queen was already looking down at some papers she was holding and Sheysu realized there would be no goodbyes.

Aurum and Sheysu walked out of the queen's chambers together.

"We'd better get going," said Aurum, his voice filled with resignation.

Sheysu tried to make light of the situation.

"Thank you so much for doing this. It means the world to me."

"I don't have a choice. The decision has been made and I have to make the best of it."

His words made her seethe once again. "You don't have to come. I'm sure if you just said no, the queen would have to accept your refusal."

"It's not as simple as that. Now you're going to have to follow my lead closely. I need to get this whole thing over as quickly as possible and the last thing I need is some girl making silly mistakes because she's not paying attention."

"This *whole thing* as you call it, is my sister's life, and believe me, I'm as keen as you, if not more so, to find Similia as quickly as possible. My sister doesn't have much time."

"Well then, get your belongings and let's get going. What are you waiting for? We have almost a full day and we can reach Animalia before nightfall."

Sheysu turned and stormed off towards her room. He made her so angry she could scream. Her pounding footsteps echoed loudly through the corridor. From behind, Aurum shouted, "Meet you back here!"

Sheysu grunted in response. How could anyone be so insensitive? He was right about one thing. They needed to find Similia fast. Not just to find the cure for her sister, but so she wouldn't have to spend one more second with him than was necessary.

# ANIMALIA

The kingdom of Animalia stood tall before Sheysu and Aurum. They were dwarfed by the large canopy of trees and the lush, green vegetation spread out, filling their view from every angle. As they walked under the first trees, the sound transformed and echoed with the song of birds and animals. The carpet of fallen leaves crunched and rustled underfoot as they walked and the air felt heavy and thick with moisture.

Sheysu felt an odd sensation sweep through her as if she were being pulled into the jungle by an invisible hand. Raw energy coursed through her veins. Her senses became heightened; she could hear every insect and animal. A million different smells flooded her nose, but she could still distinguish between them. Survival instincts kicked in. The words "kill or be killed" kept running through her mind. Never before had she felt so alive. She smiled at the irony. Sheysu felt powerful. She wanted to bound through the jungle, climb trees, and scream at the top of her voice. These different feelings overwhelmed her all at once. She felt as if she had come home, as if she belonged— an unsettling feeling, especially since she had never been here before. The tears welled up in her eyes and she quickly wiped them away before Aurum could see. The last thing Sheysu wanted was to appear weak and give him yet another reason for doubting her ability to manage the task ahead. Suddenly there was a strange rustling and running noise in the distance. Aurum stopped, and his hand reached for the unfamiliar-looking gun on his hip, but the noise subsided into the distance.

"We had better keep our eyes and ears open," said Aurum. "No doubt the people of Animalia already know we're here. They do not take kindly to strangers wandering through their kingdom, so follow my lead closely and don't do anything silly."

Sheysu prickled at his words, but she calmed herself quickly. Since her outburst this morning, she had decided to be civil, realising that her anger would only hinder the situation.

"Have you been here before?" asked Sheysu.

"Yes, a few times. On those journeys I learnt a great deal about the people of Animalia. They're a unique race who identify strongly with the animals with which they coexist. There are many different tribes and each one aligns itself to a particular animal. It's amazing really. They share the characteristics of their tribal animal and the children are inherently born with its traits. It's not as extreme as running around on all fours, but they do share the thinking and behaviour of their tribal animal. Their senses and physical strength are also influenced. Some tribes are extremely agile, such as those following monkeys, and others are cunning and deadly, such as those aligned with snakes.

Sometimes, children are born into tribes where they do not share an affinity for their tribe's chosen animal. Apparently, the mother knows this when she is carrying the child. At its birth, the tribe holds a welcome ceremony where they invite the tribe of the child's chosen animal. Sometimes the mothers find this a very difficult process and find it hard to let go, but it is a sacred ritual that goes back for centuries and is strictly adhered to. The children usually find it less difficult and instinctively go to their new tribe without fuss."

"What an interesting race. My father told me bits and pieces about them, but it's hard to imagine as they are so different from anything I've ever known."

She wanted to know everything about the Animalians, but just as she was about to ask another question, her senses tingled. Before she knew what she was doing, she launched herself at Aurum, bulldozing him with all her strength, bringing them both to the ground with a heavy thud a short distance away.

"What the...!" Aurum exclaimed as he hit the ground. Behind them came the loud sound of rumbling and crashing. They both looked over to see the ground where they had been standing collapse.

Sheysu jumped up hurriedly, realising that she was sprawled over Aurum. He sat up looking confused. "How did you know?" he asked.

Sheysu shook her head. "I didn't. I just got this strange feeling, and before I knew it, I was pushing you over."

Aurum got to his feet, brushing the dust off his

clothes. They both walked to the edge of the large, gaping hole that had appeared, and looked down into its eerie depths. It was deep, about thirty feet. At the bottom something strange glistened. They couldn't quite make it out. Aurum pulled a thin metal tube from his belt and shook it hard. It shone a powerful light, which he directed at the bottom of the hole. Sheysu gasped in horror. Rows upon rows of sharpened, pointed rocks lay at the bottom, resembling the teeth of a savage beast. The rocks shone with some kind of yellow, liquid coating.

Aurum shook his head and let out a long breath. "As I said before, Animalians do not welcome strangers into their kingdom. These rocks were meant to kill, and to make sure no one escaped, they've been coated with some kind of animal venom."

A shudder went through Sheysu as an image of them lying in the hole, all bloody and broken, flashed through her mind.

"This is more sophisticated than the traps they've used in the past. They've found a way of suspending the earth so it looks untouched. We really will have to keep on our toes, literally."

Aurum put his hands on Sheysu's shoulders and turned her to face him. His turquoise eyes stared deeply into hers. He smiled. "Thank you for saving my life, especially since it's me who should be saving yours." He chuckled.

There was a new warmth in his gaze—thankful, yes, but was there a look of admiration too?

Sheysu looked down quickly, feeling herself

blush and mumbled, "You're welcome. I really didn't know what I was doing anyway."

Aurum looked up through the trees. "It's getting dark. We'd better find somewhere to camp for the night."

They walked until they found a clearing. "I'll get wood for a fire while you look through the supplies and see what's for supper." He shrugged out of his backpack and threw a bag from it towards Sheysu. "You've got the rest of the food in your backpack," he said and walked into the trees.

Sheysu glanced around nervously, realising she was on her own. Her earlier feelings of strength and confidence in the jungle seemed to have dissipated. It really was getting very dark and she felt as if eyes were watching her from beyond the trees. She tried to shrug the feeling off so she could concentrate on getting the food out. Inside the bag Aurum had thrown her were several packets all wrapped and sealed. There were names on the packages but they meant little to her. At home she had done very little cooking; her mother had done most of that. She panicked. What would Aurum think if she couldn't even get the right food out? Pulling open her own backpack, she breathed a sigh of relief. Inside, there was bread, chicken, rice, fruit, all packaged in clear wrappings. She took out the chicken and rice and some fruit. As she laid out a blanket to put the food on, branches crunched behind her. She jumped up, startled, only to relax when she saw Aurum walking towards her, carrying a bundle of sticks.

"Good, you've got the food out." He proceeded to put the sticks in a pile. He gathered some dry leaves and then pulled two small thin tubes from his belt. From one he poured some sticky liquid onto the leaves, then shook some powdery dark crystals over it from the other. Immediately, there was a whooshing noise and flames shot up from the leaves. He fanned the flames under the pile of sticks and very quickly there was the satisfying crackle and smell of burning wood. Sheysu watched intently. She had never seen fire being made in this way, although she had heard that those living in Mineralia were very advanced and had all sorts of strange and wonderful tools and methods.

Aurum took a circular piece of flat metal out of his backpack. He tapped its sides, which then extended upwards forming a pot of sorts. Next, he grabbed the food and proceeded to add the rice to the pot, followed by water from his flask, and then put the chicken on top. From one of the packages Sheysu had been unable to decipher, he extracted a small sachet and sprinkled its contents over the pot. Sheysu realised that at least one of the packages contained some kind of seasoning. He tapped the pot again and a lid extended from one side and covered the contents. From his backpack he took two smaller discs which, when tapped became mugs. He filled these with water and handed one to Sheysu.

"Thank you," said Sheysu, mesmerised by the transforming pot and mugs.

He sat on the ground next to the fire and turned

to look at Sheysu. "The food will take a while, so now is as good a time as any for me to find out more about you."

"What do you want to know?" Sheysu asked, unable yet again to meet his gaze.

"I can't place you. You come from Planta but you don't look like anyone I've ever seen from there."

"Everybody says that," replied Sheysu and proceeded to tell Aurum the story of how she was found.

"Ah, that explains a lot, but it still doesn't help me figure out where you're from."

Sheysu looked up wistfully at the night sky and sighed. "I wish I knew that too."

"You've had a lot to deal with in a short space of time. I'm sorry if I didn't appear very helpful when we first met, but I was having troubles of my own. Leaving Mineralia, even for a short time, is going to make them worse, which is why I was so reluctant to come with you. Believe me, it's nothing personal."

Sheysu looked up to meet his gaze, saw the honesty in his eyes, and hoped she could trust him. She had been so wrapped up in her own dilemmas that it had not occurred to her, for even one second, that his resistance to helping her was because of problems of his own. She felt relieved it was not about her, but at the same time felt guilty that she had made his problems worse.

"What will happen while you are away?" asked Sheysu.

Aurum sighed, and his shoulders drooped as if

carrying a heavy weight. "What do you know about Queen Platina?"

Sheysu recounted the various bits of information she had heard about the queen's upbringing, her marriage, and the subsequent events leading to her becoming the ruler of Mineralia.

"Well that's a good start," said Aurum. "What you don't know is that I'm the late king's nephew and was next in line when he died. Queen Platina, with her manipulative ways, managed to convince the elders it was in the best interests of Mineralia to allow her to rule while I gained experience under her. She never had any intention of giving up her crown. Shortly before coming here, I suggested that now was a good time for me to become king. She agreed wholeheartedly and said she would put the necessary wheels into motion. I knew it was too easy, that she had something else planned. Your dilemma gave her the perfect excuse to get me out of the way. My worry is that while I'm gone, she'll somehow manage to convince the elders that Mineralia is better under her rule, and perhaps even change the constitutional laws to make it her rightful throne. If she was a good leader, I'd have no desire to be king, but Mineralia has done nothing but suffer since she came to power. My desire to be king is only so I can help my people."

"But, surely the elders know what she's up to."

"They do, but they are all frightened of her and what she can do to them and their families. The queen can be very vindictive. If I hadn't come with you, there's no doubt in my mind she would have taken it out on my mother and the rest of my family."

"Oh, I didn't realise. I'm sorry I took you away from Mineralia."

"It's not your fault. My hands were tied. I couldn't have gone against the queen's decision, and she would've found one way or another to remove me. We'll just have to find Similia as quickly as possible so I can get back sooner than she is expecting, and perhaps have the element of surprise on my side."

"Finding Similia is not going to be easy. I still don't understand what the queen was saying about using your intuition and letting Similia come to you. Do you?" asked Sheysu.

"I've heard many stories about Similia. Those who claim to have been successful in finding him all said the same thing: remove doubt and trust he will appear."

"Whew, that's a tall order. So do you think it means we should just carry on our journey with confidence and expect him to appear or something like that?"

Aurum nodded. "I think we should give it a go."

Sheysu's stomach rumbled as the delicious smell of food wafted past her.

Aurum leant towards the pot and sniffed the air. "I think the food should be ready." He tapped the pot and the lid retracted. From his bag he took two more metal discs, which became plates after he tapped them. He spooned some chicken and rice onto a plate and handed it to Sheysu together with a spoon. It looked and smelled so good. They ate quickly in silence, both obviously very hungry.

It was getting very late and they had to make an early start, so Aurum gathered the pots and plates and disappeared to clean them. Her full stomach and the heat from the fire made her drowsy. She yawned, making a big stretch and walked over to her backpack. From it she detached the sleeping bag and shook it out, laying it in front of the fire. She half got into the sleeping bag and watched for Aurum's return with eyes slowly growing heavier and heavier.

*She looked up to see Aurum coming through the trees towards her. There was something different about him. His eyes had changed to onyx pebbles and all the warmth had disappeared. He glided rather than walked. Something was very wrong. Aurum's face started to change and his arms melted into his trunk while his legs merged to become one. Very slowly, his head and body moved closer to the floor until he was sliding, almost undulating towards her. He was closer now and had become one long, sinuous body covered in large, black, diamond-shaped markings. Sheysu wanted to run, but her body was frozen with terror. What was happening and what had Aurum become? Only a few feet from her now, his pointed, triangular head reared up and a loud hiss echoed from his opening mouth. A tongue, a forked tongue, emerged, darting quickly in and out. His mouth opened wider than seemed possible and Sheysu screamed when she saw large fangs emerge as his head lunged towards her. In that second just before he struck, awareness hit her that Aurum had become an enormous snake. She heard herself scream, but then, instead of the expected pain, she felt herself being shaken.*

"Sheysu wake up!"

She flung her eyes open and saw the familiar

Aurum bent over her, concern in his eyes. "You were having a bad dream. I heard you screaming just as I was coming back."

Sheysu looked at Aurum, still frightened but now disorientated as well. It slowly dawned on her that she'd been having a nightmare. She breathed a huge sigh of relief, but couldn't shake off the feeling of cold terror gripping her. The dream had been so real. What did it mean? Was Aurum out to get her? No, she couldn't believe that. She realised she was not feeling well. She was lying with the sleeping bag pulled tightly up around her neck. Suddenly, it felt like it was suffocating her. The cloth around her neck felt oppressive. She grabbed it and pulled it down, feeling relief as the night air cooled her down.

"Why were you screaming?" asked Aurum.

Sheysu didn't know what to say, she was too embarrassed to say the dream was about him attacking her as a snake. Instead, she said, "I really can't remember."

Even though the cool air helped, she still felt unwell. Camphora's words echoed in her mind. *"You too will begin to feel some of her symptoms."* Could this be it? Was she now experiencing her sister's illness? She panicked as four weeks now seemed like such a short time. She realised Aurum was watching her, so she quickly wiped the anxiety from her face and pretended to yawn. "I think I'm going to try to get more sleep. It's been an eventful day."

"Goodnight," said Aurum, looking at her, unconvinced.

Ignoring his look, she turned over, facing away from him, and closed her eyes. Sheysu lay quietly, hoping sleep would come quickly, but suspicious thoughts kept bombarding her. *Was it possible Aurum would purposefully jeopardise her quest so he could get back to Mineralia? Had the dream been a warning? He didn't have the look of a cold-blooded killer. No, she didn't believe he could do that, but maybe he would just abandon her while she slept?* That last thought made sleep even more impossible, but eventually exhaustion took over and she fell into a restless slumber.

Sheysu woke to the clatter of pans and the delicious aroma of coffee teasing her nose. It was still dark and she had no idea what time it was. She pulled herself into a seated position, keeping the sleeping bag around her, as the cold air pricked her skin. Aurum was busy over the fire, stirring a pot and pouring coffee into cups. He looked up at her and smiled. Relief that he was still there washed over her. A warmth spread through her and realised to her surprise that she was happy to see him.

Smiling back she said, "Good morning. What time is it?"

"It's five o' clock. I think we'd best get an early start. There's coffee and porridge if you can eat this early."

Sheysu pulled herself out of the sleeping bag and shivered while reaching for her jacket.

"I'd love some coffee. Not sure about the porridge though. I still have memories of practically being force fed the stuff when I was younger, but I'll give it a go."

Aurum handed her a cup of coffee and a bowl of unfamiliar-looking porridge. Putting down the coffee, she hesitantly sniffed a spoonful of the sticky mixture. It smelled of nothing in particular. She ate the spoonful, and memories of sitting over a bowl of porridge for what seemed an eternity, came flooding back. Ugh!! This variety tasted just as bad. It came as a bit of a shock—after dinner the previous night, she had been expecting a culinary delight. She smiled with the realisation that porridge was porridge, no matter what kingdom you came from. It was a comforting thought. Knowing she needed the energy, she put her memories away and ate the contents of the bowl as quickly as possible. The coffee, thankfully, was just what she needed and washed away any remnants of the porridge. After breakfast they packed everything away into their backpacks and headed off deeper into the jungle.

The night mist was slowly rising and rays of sunshine began to streak downwards through the tall trees. The songs of birds and other animals grew ever stronger, punctuated here and there with the deep, rumbling growl of a big cat and the piercing call of an elephant. Sheysu thought she would be frightened, but the same raw energy that pulsed through her veins yesterday was evident today. Despite the weight of her backpack, she felt light and incredibly steady on her feet, even over the rough terrain. She breathed a sigh of relief as the symptoms she had associated with her sister's illness appeared to have passed. But for how long?

# LOST

Sheysu took off her jacket and wrapped it around her waist. Droplets of sweat trickled down her body, forming an intricate network of channels. Aurum led the way, a few feet in front. He had already taken off his waistcoat and his shirt stuck to the muscular contours of his back. Sheysu scoured the jungle looking for some clue to Similia's whereabouts. Her shoulders drooped and she sighed. She had no idea what she was looking for and wondered how long they would have to aimlessly trek through the jungle before they found some kind of sign. They had been walking for some hours when Aurum turned to look at her.

"Let's stop for a rest. The heat today is unbearable and we really must find some water to keep up our strength. Give me your canteen. I'll find some."

"But it's still half full."

"Finish what's there and then I'll fill it. You need to drink more. We can't have you fainting from dehydration."

Sheysu nodded, pulled out her canteen, and gulped down its contents.

"Wait here by this tree, and I'll be back shortly." He gestured towards the tree next to him.

"I'll come with you."

Aurum's gaze drifted over her and he shook his head. "No, you look tired and you need the rest. I won't be long."

Sheysu brushed the area at the base of the tree with her foot to clear away any insects, and then sat down against it, sighing with relief at its welcome support. She watched Aurum disappear into the bushes and then surveyed her surroundings. Looking back and forth, she realised that every direction she looked appeared identical. She couldn't even tell which part of the jungle they had just come from. The huge, fearsome snake from her dream flashed through her mind. Could this be it? Could this be the opportunity that Aurum had been waiting for to abandon her and return to Mineralia? She looked around and noticed that he had not left his bag. Her mind began racing. Why would he take the extra weight of his bag to go and collect water? Unable to rest, she jumped to her feet and paced up and down anxiously.

Tentatively, she called out, "Aurum?"

Birds flapped away nearby, disturbed by her voice, but no other reply was forthcoming. She couldn't just wait here. As much as she hated to admit it, she needed his help. She would go after him and try to change his mind. At least she remembered which way he took, and began running in that direction. After several minutes, she was exhausted from the heat. She stopped and bent over, supporting herself with her hands on her thighs. Panting, she raised her head to view her surroundings and with dismay noticed that once again everything looked the same. She whirled around in panic. Which direction had she come from?

Fear rose within her and in a frightened, shaking voice she shouted, "Aurum, where are you?" Again no reply.

Like her first day in Animalia, she could hear everything, but this time it was as if she were being bombarded by a cacophony of jungle sounds. Her head was full of noise and she looked around wildly. To escape the blare, she ran on blindly, but the din would not be quieted.

Horrified at the thought of being lost in the jungle, she shouted in her loudest voice, "Aurum, please help me!" She waited, wondering if she should keep moving. The bushes to her left began to rustle. She saw the foliage move as if something huge were coming towards her. The rustling got louder. Terrified at what it could be, she ran to the nearest tree and began to climb.

"What the hell are you doing!"

She turned to see Aurum looking up at her, red-faced with anger.

"This journey is difficult enough without you galavanting off. You could've been killed. Don't you get it?"

"I... I thought you had left me. That you were on your way back to Mineralia. I was trying to find you to change your mind."

Aurum screwed up his face in disbelief. "Of all the crazy ideas. What on earth made you think that?"

"It's not so crazy. You said you needed to get back as quickly as possible. That you needed to help Mineralia. That sending you on this trip was Queen Platina's attempt to get you out of the way. On top of that, why would you take your heavy bag to collect water?"

"Yes, I did say those things. But, I also agreed to come and help you, and believe me, my word is my bond. I've had many opportunities to leave you if I had wanted to do. Why would I wait till now? I took my bag because I have extra drinking vessels in it and tools if I needed to dig."

"Oh. I know it doesn't make sense. I realise that now. I just panicked. I'm sorry." She climbed down, her limbs jelly-like from relief.

Aurum sighed. "Look, Sheysu. If we are going to get through this, you have to do what I tell you. You have to trust me. I don't have time for this."

"I know. I'm sorry. It won't happen again."

"Okay then." Aurum let out a long breath before continuing. "When I couldn't find you, it occurred to me that you wouldn't be able to survive in the jungle alone. So, I think it's best if I teach you some survival skills while we're searching for Similia."

Sheysu nodded, still trembling from her ordeal.

"We may as well start your first lesson now. I heard you shouting before I could collect some water. So let's do that first. Did you ever have to look for water in Planta?"

"No, we had a well."

"Our best bet is to find water in the plants

nearby. Bamboo or thick vines are usually the most promising. Bamboo grows in damper areas. Over there, can you see that the ground looks moist and almost boggy?" Aurum pointed to the left, where he had come from.

Sheysu looked over to see that the ground was just as Aurum described. He led her in that direction, cutting some of the vegetation he had emerged from to make a pathway for them to walk through. The air became damp and the earth soft. Once through the bushes, they entered a small clearing where thick bamboo grew in abundance to one side.

"Here." Aurum put his knife back into its sheath and handed it to her. "Tap the bamboo and see if you can figure out where the water is."

Sheysu took the knife, still in a daze after her fright, and walked towards the bamboo, her eyes searching for clues. She tapped the tall stems in various places, but it all sounded the same, a hollow echo. She found it difficult to concentrate and had no idea what she was doing, so she glanced round at Aurum. His face gave nothing away while he waited patiently. *Was it a trick question?* She tapped some more and found that lower down on some of the bamboo, the sound was denser.

Sheysu touched the denser sounding areas tentatively. "Here, maybe?"

"Good." His earlier anger seemed to have dissipated and Sheysu exhaled loudly, relieved that she had gotten it right.

"Use the knife," Aurum instructed Sheysu, "to

scrape away the brown covering so no hairs get into the water, then cut a notch just above the bamboo joint, and hold your canteen below, ready to catch the water." He handed Sheysu her canteen.

She pulled the knife from its sheath and began scraping away the brown, hairy, protective sleeve of the bamboo stem. She then carefully carved a small hole out of the exposed woody surface. As soon as she had pierced through the thickness of the bamboo, a thin jet of water sprayed out. She widened the hole and was amazed to see a steady flow of water, which she just managed to catch in her canteen. A couple more notches in other bamboo stems and her canteen was full. She looked up at Aurum and smiled with the delight of a young child.

"Well, you've done such a good job that you can fill mine too." Aurum smiled back and handed her his canteen. She reached for it, her fingers brushing his. She shivered at the touch. For a second their eyes met, both still smiling, their fingers still touching. Sheysu felt her cheeks grow hot and she turned her gaze away, feeling confused. She pulled the canteen from his hand and pretended to busy herself with getting more water.

For that day and the next, they continued their trek through the jungle with Aurum stopping every now and then to teach Sheysu a new skill. By the time the sun was lowering on the second day, she had learnt many survival skills including how to identify which insects were safe to eat if she were desperate, and how to use a stick and its shadow in the sun to get her bearings. Aurum was a surprisingly good teacher and she was amazed at how much he knew. But his seemingly endless knowledge also made her feel inadequate. He didn't leave her as she had feared, and whilst she knew he was not happy to be there, he appeared to be making the best of it. Eventually, they stopped that night at a clearing. Aurum was about to light a fire when a fat raindrop landed on Sheysu's cheek. She looked up and more drops fell and trickled down her face. Within seconds the few drops became a deluge and her hair was soon plastered to her head.

"Let's get under those trees!" shouted Aurum as he ran in the now-deafening downpour. Sheysu followed and they were soon sheltered from the worst of the rain by the fan of branches and leaves that spread out above them.

"We'll have to build a shelter for tonight," said Aurum. "This rain doesn't look like it's stopping any time soon. It'll be another good survival lesson for you. The first thing we need is a long pole. Look for a dead branch at least as thick as your arm."

Sheysu scanned the area while Aurum began hacking off lower branches from the tree above them. She spotted a long branch on the ground a short distance away and ran towards it, ploughing through the sheets of rain. Close up it looked about the right thickness and length. She picked up one end and began dragging it back towards Aurum. The mud underfoot was slippery and before she could react, her feet flew up in the air and she landed on her bottom with a thud. Dazed from the fall, she sat there for a few seconds and then scrambled to get to her feet, but ended up running on the spot as the slimy earth slipped away from underneath her. Finally, almost standing again, she steadied herself with her arms outstretched and then carefully grabbed the branch and tried to take another step. As she tugged the branch, she flew forward and fell to the ground, her face landing squarely in the mud with a squelch. She lifted her face out of the thick sludge, and was greeted by the sound of laughter. Wiping her eyes, she saw that Aurum, instead of coming to her aid, was shaking with his hand over his mouth, trying to suppress his laugh. Pulling herself up to a seated position, she was about to get angry, but then realised how ridiculous she must look, and began chuckling too. They stayed like that for a few moments, Aurum freeing his laughter and Sheysu laughing so hard she could hardly catch her breath. For those brief seconds all her worries and pain were forgotten, washed away like the slurry sliding down her face.

Eventually, Aurum came over, still laughing, and helped Sheysu up. He grabbed the branch and towed it with them. Back under the cover of the tree, he gently wiped the remnants of dirt from her face with soft, slow strokes. He ran his fingers through her hair, loosening the caked mud from between the tendrils and then shook them free. Sheysu blushed at his touch, yet she couldn't bring herself to pull away, her skin tingling in a trail that followed his fingers. He continued for what seemed an eternity but then abruptly, he coughed and pulled away. Hurriedly, he began to demonstrate how to build a shelter. Sheysu looked on with feigned concentration, her thoughts lingering over what had just happened.

With the shelter built, Aurum managed to make a small fire and began cooking the same dinner as on their first night. The rain eased off in its intensity and they sat in the shelter with the sound of the rain gently tapping against its roof of branches and leaves. While they waited for the food to cook, Aurum sat down beside Sheysu. "The food won't be much longer. You mentioned that you and your sister are twins. I've always wondered—what's it like growing up with a twin?"

"Well, I don't know any different really. I suppose we've always had each other, which was really helpful, especially when we were picked on by the other children."

"How did you cope?"

"We used to go away on our own and build fantasy worlds where no one could be cruel to us. Kora loved snakes, and where we lived there were lots of non-poisonous ones. She used to catch them and we kept them as pets. We built little caves and dwellings for them and caught bugs and mice to feed them. They always managed to escape, so we'd have to start again. Still, that was part of the fun. Looking back, I think I enjoyed it as much as she did.

"I could think of many other animals that I'd rather keep as pets."

"Most people would say the same thing, and I used to think that too. But once I started playing with snakes, I changed my mind. I just found them fascinating: the texture of their skin, their movements, the way they look at you so intensely. That's only the little non-poisonous ones, though. I still find the venomous ones terrifying. " Sheysu remembered her dream once more and a wave of fear shook through her.

After dinner, Aurum talked about growing up in Mineralia. He soon had her howling with laughter as he regaled her with stories of his childhood antics—hiding in the palace and playing pranks on the various pompous dignitaries who passed through. After their difficult start together, Sheysu couldn't believe how easy she now felt in his company. As he recounted the stories, the weight of his troubles with Mineralia appeared to lift and Sheysu found she couldn't take her eyes away from the warmth and humour radiating from his now-relaxed face. She could have watched and listened to him all night.

When he started clearing up, Sheysu sat in front of the fire with a sense of disappointment that their evening had ended. That feeling surprised her. Only a couple of days ago she had been doubtful of Aurum's motives, but he hadn't left as she had feared. Instead he had become her teacher and ally. Could she now trust him?

# A RIVER RUNS THROUGH ANIMALIA

The sound of rushing water grew louder and louder. The trees cleared before them, framing a river weaving its way between the many boulders standing in its path. Sheysu walked from underneath the cover of the trees, where the unfettered rays of the sun enveloped her in all their warmth. She stood face upwards, eyes closed, for a long pause, taking in all that was around her: the bubbling river, the clean air washed by the river beneath, and the soft blanket of the sun's rays. Sheysu was unaware of Aurum watching her until his cough startled her. She looked across at him. He was staring at her with the same look he'd had when she saved him, and as their eyes met, he quickly looked away.

"We'll have to cross the river. It runs through the entire length of Animalia. It looks deceptively shallow." Aurum walked across to a nearby tree and with his sharp knife cut off two straight-looking branches. He trimmed the offshoots as he walked towards her, and handed her one of the sticks.

"Use this to help steady yourself as you cross. Keep your backpack loose in case you need to take it off in a hurry so it doesn't drag you down. Look out for debris that could knock you over. Follow my lead closely as it gets pretty deep in the middle."

Sheysu had never liked being in water and both she and her sister had never followed the other children when they splashed and swum in the lakes near their home. She didn't enjoy the prospect of getting in the water now. Anxiety fluttered wildly in her stomach.

"Surely there must be a bridge somewhere along its length?" she asked.

"The river runs right through, and the Animalians like it that way. It makes it harder for strangers to enter their kingdom, and gives them some protection. The other sides of Animalia are enclosed by a formidable mountain range. It wouldn't make sense for them to build a bridge."

Aurum must have sensed her anxiety and gently said, "Don't be afraid. We'll get through it. Just stick close to me."

Forgetting their truce-like camaraderie, Sheysu mistook his reassuring words as pointing out her weaknesses. "Of course we'll get through it. I'm not afraid. I was just looking for an easier option. I'll be perfectly fine, thank you." With that, she set off towards the river's edge, not looking back to see if Aurum was following.

The smooth boulders near the river's edge were slippery and hard to navigate. Sheysu was thankful for the stick that steadied her more than once, even before she reached the water. She could hear Aurum's footsteps behind her and relaxed. For all her bravado, she really was glad he was with her. Tentatively, she took her first steps into the water. It felt cold through her boots as she waded in slowly, each footstep splashing and growing heavier as the water deepened. *It really wasn't too bad*, she thought, and began to relax, her pace quickening and becoming more confident.

Very soon, she had almost reached the middle. The water was now waist deep and she could no longer make out what she was stepping on. She slowed at this point as she felt her way along gingerly, her feet nudging forward cautiously, feeling for firm ground for the next step. The river began to creep past her shoulders and she did not relish the thought of swimming in such a strong current. Sheysu was beginning to wish she hadn't taken the lead and turned her head to see Aurum about ten feet behind her. Should she wait for him? She was toying with the idea when, without warning, the ground she thought was solid gave way beneath her feet, submerging her. Disorientated and panicking, she tried to push herself up towards the surface, but her feet had become entangled in something. She could hear Aurum's muffled voice above the water calling her name. Using all her energy, she pulled hard against her entrapment and broke free from the river bed with such force that she lost all balance. The powerful current carried her away and, whilst she had broken free, whatever had entangled her was still wrapped around her feet, tying them firmly together. Water gushed into her nose and invaded her mouth. She struggled to get her head above water, coughing and spluttering, and took in a short breath.

The current pulled stronger and Sheysu flailed along like a rag doll. Without the use of her feet, it was almost impossible to keep her head out of water, so she reached down and tried in vain to pull off whatever had tied her feet together, but its grip was firm and unrelenting. Panic took hold of her when, out of nowhere, she heard her sister saying, *"You must survive."* The words made her focus, and with a super-human effort, she raised her head above water to take a long breath, opening her eyes for just long enough to see Aurum swimming towards her. Reaching out, she tried frantically to grab anything she could to slow down. Her fingertips brushed the branch of a tree tantalisingly close, but frustratingly she couldn't get a grip. Once more she became submerged, and once more she used every ounce of her energy to get another breath.

There were boulders all around her and she narrowly avoided hitting them, but only by sheer fluke as she had no real control over where she was going. The backpack strapped to her shoulders was weighing her down, and remembering what Aurum had said, she pulled it off and let it go, affording her a little more buoyancy. Her energy began to wane and she didn't know how much longer she could muster the strength to keep lifting her head above water. Something touched her waist, and then it pulled her hard. She looked up, frightened, and then relaxed when she saw Aurum's face. She could have wept with joy. Holding her close, he managed to pull them towards the shore. He dragged her unceremoniously out of the water, but she didn't care. She had survived! They collapsed in a heap on the ground. She trembled from shock and the cold. Aurum tightened his arm around her to keep her warm, but he was wet too. Relief filled every pore of her body. Feeling safe in his arms, she realised in that moment that this was where she wanted to be.

"I thought I'd lost you," said Aurum. "You disappeared so quickly. I should never have let you go first." His voice was heavy with guilt.

"It's not your fault, Aurum. It was my own wounded pride and stubbornness that nearly got me killed. Next time I will listen to you, I promise."

"Even so, I shouldn't have let you go ahead. It was my responsibility to ensure your safety. It won't happen again." His face was tight with anger at himself.

"Don't be so hard on yourself. Look at it this way, we are even now—a life for a life."

He managed to muster up a weak, unconvincing smile. "The sun will be setting soon. We'd better make a fire and get dry." Aurum moved as if to get up and then noticed Sheysu's feet. "No wonder you couldn't swim to shore."

He pulled a knife out of his belt and cut the vine-like plant that had bound her feet together so tightly. Sheysu stretched in relief and stood, glad to have the use of her legs back. Her clothes were not as wet as she would have thought; the fabric was drying quickly.

Her teeth chattered with the cold and she looked forward to the fire Aurum mentioned.

Aurum turned to look back towards the jungle. "Let's find a sheltered spot to make camp, not too far from the river. I think we've had enough excitement for today."

They walked for a couple of minutes through the dense foliage and found a small clearing.

Aurum shrugged out of his backpack and handed it to her. "I'll get some wood for a fire and you see what there is to eat."

"What are we going to do for food? My backpack, it's gone. I had to get rid of it."

"I know. I saw it floating off. It was the right thing to do. The food in the backpacks was only meant to keep us going for about a week, so sooner or later, we were going to have to fend for ourselves. It's just a bit sooner, that's all. There should be enough for some kind of meal in my bag for tonight. Tomorrow, well, that's another story. If we're near the river, then fish may be on the menu."

Sheysu had a feeling of déjà vu as she opened Aurum's backpack and hunted for food, but at least this time, she had some idea of what each package contained. Thankfully, he had mixed up supplies from the two bags over the past couple of days. There was fruit, some bread, and at the bottom, she found what looked like a large piece of cheese. *Great,* she thought, *it's not hot but it will definitely keep us going.* Aurum had the discs for pots in his bag, so at least they would be able to make some coffee. She pulled out Aurum's sleeping bag, which was amazingly dry thanks to some kind of protective covering. Sheysu spread it on the ground and set the food on it. Aurum came back carrying sticks for the fire and, just like the day before, he made fire using liquid and crystals.

The heat from the fire grew quickly and melted the coldness from her body. Sheysu stood close to it and removed her boots so her trousers could dry. She wanted to take her clothes off, but since her backpack was gone, she had nothing else to cover up with. At that moment, as if reading her mind, Aurum pulled a shirt from his bag. "Here, get out of those wet clothes and put this on."

Sheysu took the shirt gratefully and went behind a tree to get undressed. She removed her trousers which were nearly dry, but just as she was taking off her shirt, she felt eyes watching her. Looking up, she saw Aurum had his back to her and was still tending the fire. She turned and stared hard into the darkening jungle. Bushes moved and she concentrated her gaze more intently, but saw nothing. Yet she still sensed someone was there. A shiver ran up her back and she quickly made her way to Aurum. She walked back self-consciously as his shirt only reached her mid-thigh. Aurum looked up as he heard her approach; she blushed as his eyes lingered. He turned away quickly and busied himself with putting food out on plates. Sheysu had never thought of herself as being particularly attractive and was unaware of how striking she looked with the contrast of her olive skin against the crisp white shirt.

The smell of coffee filled the air. She could

almost taste the thick, nutty liquid, and shivered in anticipation.

"What about your clothes? They must be wet too," asked Sheysu.

"Don't worry about me. This is nothing, and anyway, they are practically dry. A couple of hours in front of the fire and I'll be fine."

She spread her clothes out on a low branch a short distance from the fire so they could dry. When she finished, Aurum handed her a cup of hot coffee. It smelled so good. Sheysu cradled it between her hands, letting the warmth permeate her body, and breathed in deeply to capture the smoky aroma, as she sat on the sleeping bag, which was comfortingly warm from the heat of the fire.

Aurum extended a plate of food towards her and sat down at the other end of the sleeping bag, facing her with his plate of food.

Sheysu wanted to know more about Aurum and Mineralia.

"What's life like in Mineralia now?"

"Before Queen Platina took over, there was harmony, order, and structure. Like the parts of a clock, everything synchronised beautifully. The community was strong and provided support for all. Children were nurtured, not just by their families, but by the whole community. Everyone worked together to make a whole. What was lacking in one was complemented by another. When Queen Platina took over, the structure of Mineralia, which had been so finely honed with such precision, collapsed. It was as if everything we had always known and cherished literally came crashing down around us. Life spiralled out of control into a fathomless abyss. Families and whole communities fell apart. Where we had been together, we were now separate and opposed. She created a life of servitude to the palace, breeding fear amongst all so none would oppose. Many have left Mineralia, and those who have stayed have been worn down with fear or are waiting and hoping for change. I never dreamt things could get so bad. I feel responsible in many ways. If only I had opposed Queen Platina more strongly when the king died, it may never have happened."

Sheysu felt the despair clinging to his words.

"Having met Queen Platina, I don't think there's anything you could've done that would have resulted in a different outcome," said Sheysu reassuringly.

"You're probably right, but I still feel responsible. It's up to me now to make sure Mineralia can have a new beginning when I get back. This time, no matter what, I won't take no for an answer. If I have to organise an uprising, so be it. There are many who will follow me, joined together with the many that will follow my bride-to-be."

Sheysu's head shot up. "Your bride-to-be?"

"Yes, it was agreed by the king shortly before his death. She is from a noble family in Mineralia. Her name is Argonisa. It is commonplace amongst the royals and aristocracy of Mineralia to have marriages arranged for them when they are young, many years before the wedding itself. Her family is a powerful one with many allies and connections in Mineralia. It is a good match for all."

"Is it a good match for you?" asked Sheysu.

"It is my duty. Mineralia comes first. We are very different. She had a difficult childhood. Her father is an extremely busy man and her mother died when she was very young, leaving her alone for most of her childhood with only the servants for company. She is however, very content, but almost lives in her own world. Argonisa doesn't seem to need anybody or anything, including me. That suits me. At least that way there is no pretence it is anything other than a marriage of convenience."

"How can you marry without love?" Sheysu hesitated. "Sorry, that's none of my business."

"No, no, it's okay, Sheysu. I don't believe in fairy tales. Mineralia is my priority. To safeguard its future, I will do whatever is necessary."

Sheysu suddenly felt very alone.

# CANIDAE

The next afternoon Sheysu had the sensation they were being followed. They had already been walking for five hours, going deeper into the jungle. An intense odour wafted across her nostrils—a familiar yet new smell, if that were possible. The scent was growing stronger.

"Can you smell that?" asked Sheysu.

"Smell what?"

Sheysu looked up, surprised. The odour was so powerful, how could he not smell it?

"I think we're being followed."

"I know," whispered Aurum. "They've been with us since we left camp this morning. I didn't want to worry you. They were keeping their distance, but now they've come closer. I can't make them out exactly, but I think there are at least six men, maybe more. If they had wanted to kill us, they would've done so by now. Here, take this." Aurum handed her a weapon similar to that on his belt.

"But I don't know how to use it and I'm not sure I want to."

"Believe me, if the time comes, you'll want to. Just twist this dial to release and then press this button to fire." He pointed at two small controls on the handle. Sheysu took the strange gun, holding it as if it would explode at any moment.

"Don't worry. It's quite safe until you twist the dial."

She put it gingerly into her belt, where it clicked in snugly, and hoped sincerely she would never have to use it.

The odour overpowered her senses now and came from all directions. Sheysu and Aurum stopped abruptly as two men emerged from the bushes in front of them. More men appeared from all sides, about ten in all. They held long spears but pointed them downwards, not at Sheysu and Aurum. Aurum put his arm protectively around Sheysu and pulled her close.

All the men wore knee-length shorts made from rough fabric, tied around the waist with a scarf-like belt. They had leather straps over their bare shoulders holding knives and other weapons. Different headdresses were worn by some, whilst others had none. The headdresses were intricate—woven from fabric, plants, and stones—and resembled animal heads with stones for eyes and teeth. One of the men in front stepped forward. He had an ornate headdress and was powerfully built. He stared intently at Aurum. Abruptly, Aurum moved towards him, letting go of Sheysu. She looked round nervously to see the other men raise their spears in an aggressive stance. The man in front waved his hands down, gesturing to the others. They lowered their spears.

A smile began to form on his face. "Aurum?" he asked.

Aurum moved forward again and shook the man's hand.

"It is you, Lupinum? I nearly didn't recognise you. It must be, what, five years since I saw you last?"

"Five years, maybe more. So what brings you to Animalia after all this time, and who is your companion?" asked Lupinum

Sheysu realised all eyes were on her. Lupinum was looking at her with a keenly curious expression.

"This is Sheysu. Her sister is very sick and I am helping her find Similia."

"I am pleased to meet you, Sheysu. I am sorry to hear your sister is unwell. Where have you travelled from?"

He leant forward as if to make sure that he could hear her answer clearly.

"Planta. I have been travelling for a few days now."

"Planta? Were you travelling from somewhere else before?"

"I know, I don't look as if I come from there. It's a long story."

"An intriguing one by the sounds of it. Maybe you could share it with us over a meal tonight. I insist you both come to our village to rest and refresh yourselves. Aurum, we have much to catch up. It's been a long time. Maybe we can also be of service in helping you find Similia."

This was good news. At last there could be some solid clues in finding Similia. Since her conversation with Aurum last night, she had been feeling distinctly low. This news made her heart race and lifted her spirits.

Sheysu smiled. "That would be wonderful, thank you."

Aurum nodded. "Yes, that would be great. Our food supplies are running a bit low."

"Our village is a couple of miles from here. I have some urgent business to attend to, so we will have to race back. I will leave my tribesman, Cain Lac, to guide you at a more leisurely pace."

A young man with no headdress stepped forward from behind Sheysu and Aurum. He was maybe a year or two younger than Sheysu. His skin was a rich shade of copper brown. He was not as powerfully built as Lupinum, but was lean and muscular nonetheless.

Lupinum gestured to the other tribesman, and with a quick wave to Aurum, he was off, racing at incredible speed with the others through the bushes. Having never seen anyone move so fast before, Sheysu was astounded at their rapid pace. She remembered what Aurum had said about Animalians possessing the traits of the animals they aligned themselves to.

Cain Lac started walking in the direction the others had taken, not saying a word. Aurum and Sheysu began following. Sheysu turned to Aurum.

"What tribe are they from?"

"The Canidae. Their tribe follows the Canidae family which includes wolves, dogs, jackals and coyotes."

"That explains why they could run so fast." Sheysu wondered what urgent matter had made

Lupinum and the others run off in such haste. Could it have anything to do with finding them? Would they really help her as Lupinum had said or was Cain leading them into some kind of trap?

# CAIN LAC

Something wasn't right but Cain couldn't put his finger on it. They had followed the unknown couple since this morning and had not attacked under direct orders from Lupinum. Ordinarily, strangers were captured at the very least. Cain knew there was something different about these two. The female had a strong scent not unlike their own Canidae scent, but it was different. They had not come across a scent so similar before. Lupinum was curious, so they followed the pair to see what they would do. The girl was attractive and Cain found her alluring to say the least, so was not averse to following them. But it had been an uneventful journey; they just kept walking deeper into the jungle.

After five hours of keeping a distance, Lupinum decided it was time to make their presence known. It turned out Lupinum knew the man, Aurum, a Mineralian. The word made Cain shudder. He did not like Mineralians. In fact, he hated them. The girl was different though. Sheysu was her name. Lupinum had reacted strangely when he spoke to her. Something about her had agitated him so much he decided to rush back to the village before them. Lupinum had left

Cain to take the couple back to the village. He was disappointed he had been left behind, but he was used to it. He could not oppose Lupinum's orders, especially since he was the Omega of the tribe, the dogsbody, and Lupinum was the son of the chief. Cain was eager to get back, to find out what was going on, but he couldn't bring himself to talk to the Mineralian, so he just started walking, knowing they would follow. He increased his pace so they could get back quickly. He heard the couple talking. Sheysu seemed very interested in finding out about Cain's tribe. Aurum explained the make-up of their tribe and Cain grimaced with disgust at his simplified description. What could a Mineralian possibly know about the complexities of life as a Canidae?

It took them just under half an hour to reach the village. Their tribe was large and many tent-like wooden structures dotted a large clearing. Many more tents lay camouflaged by the jungle. In the centre of the village stood the Elders' tent. This is where Lupinum would've gone.

Cain turned to Sheysu and said, "Wait here." He ran into the Elders' tent. The Alpha—the chief of the tribe, Lupus Canis, who was Lupinum's father—sat at the back of the tent, facing the entrance. The Elders, who were previous chiefs or older relatives, sat next to him, forming a circle. There were seven in all. Lupinum stood to the left, addressing them. No one looked up as Cain entered. They were used to him coming and going, bringing food and drink. Lupinum was speaking.

"Should we tell her?"

"No, not yet," one of the Elders spoke. "We don't know if this story about looking for Similia is really true. If it is, we must help her. Let us observe her until we are sure it is safe to tell her. Her return will have a great impact on the tribe."

"Are we certain it is her? We can't risk making a mistake," said another Elder.

"Yes," said Lupinum. "Her scent is unmistakable. She can be no other than Aureus's daughter."

Cain felt the words envelop him in a heavy black cloud. Aureus… The name reverberated in his head. She had been responsible for his father's fate and was the cause of his family's relegation to the Omega status within the tribe. Whilst growing up, he had seen his father ravaged by the bitterness and injustice of being cheated of his destiny, all because of one woman: Aureus. She had long since disappeared, but now her daughter, of all people, had returned. Returned for what? He felt an immense rage rise through his body. It was as if a dam had burst. All the anger he had felt over the years from being looked down upon, the resulting feelings of worthlessness, of never being good enough, suddenly had an outlet, a direction: Sheysu. He would make her pay for what her family had done to his. Cain wanted her to suffer and know the humiliation he and his father had been subjected to.

# THE CANIDAE VILLAGE

Sheysu stood awkwardly with Aurum in the centre of the village where Cain had left them, aware of the many probing eyes now on them. Shuffling nervously, she found it difficult to meet their curious gazes. It was if their spiky stares were poking and digging into her. In an attempt to appear relaxed, she looked around casually, trying not to make eye contact. The women looked vaguely familiar. Some of them had wavy hair, not unlike her own but much longer. Their clothing was made of the same fabric as the men's, but was wrapped round their bodies tightly from their chests to their thighs. Similar to the men again, some wore headdresses whilst others had none. The same scent she had noticed when the others were following them floated heavily in the air, but not unpleasantly. She was at a loss to remember where she had encountered it before.

"Why are they all staring at me?" asked Sheysu.

Aurum raised his eyebrows. "It's not just you. It's both of us. They don't often get strangers coming through their village. We're quite the novelty."

"No I don't think it's just that. There's something else, and they are looking at me more than you. I can feel it."

Lupinum emerged from the same tent Cain had entered and his eyes met Sheysu's. There it was again—that curious, almost suspicious, look. Sheysu felt distinctly uneasy. He strode over to them.

"Welcome to our village. Pay no attention to our tribe members. You are somewhat of a novelty in these parts."

Aurum looked over at Sheysu with a smug "I told you so" look. She ignored him.

"You must be tired. Cain will show you where you can freshen up, and then please join us in the Elders' tent for some food."

He motioned to the tent he had just come from.

Sheysu looked at Cain, who was now standing a little way behind Lupinum. Confusion filled her head. She couldn't understand why, but the look Cain gave her was one of pure hatred. Diverting her gaze quickly, she wondered if she were going mad. Was this paranoia part of the sickness? She looked up again to make sure, but he was no longer staring at her. Instead, he had started walking away from them, and like before, they followed. He stopped at a large tent which was on its own, slightly away from the others and turned to Aurum.

"You can freshen up in here. When you have finished, join Lupinum in the Elders' tent." He didn't wait for any response and was almost gone before he had stopped speaking. Aurum looked at Sheysu, shrugging his shoulders as if to say "I don't know what his problem is."

Inside, the tent appeared even larger than it did from the outside. The floor looked as if it had been recently swept. At one end was a table on which there was a large, shallow bowl with a jug next to it and some towels. To the left of the table was a rug-like bed with blankets and pillows. In the middle of the tent, there was a cloth partition which Aurum lifted, and they both walked through. On the other side of the partition the rest of the tent was laid out in a mirror image of the first half.

"You freshen up in here, and I'll use the other side," said Aurum.

Aurum went back through the partition, leaving Sheysu to collect her thoughts. As she poured water from the jug into the bowl, she reflected on her meeting with the Canidae. Her sense of unease was growing. She didn't trust Lupinum. He seemed to have some ulterior motive, but what? Cain, on the other hand… Well, he was just incredibly rude, and what reason could he possibly have for hating her? Sheysu was beginning to wish they hadn't been found by the Canidae, but then she remembered Lupinum's offer of help to find Similia. She didn't know if it was genuine, but it had to be worth taking the risk. She splashed cold water on her face again and again. The water cooled her, physically and emotionally, cleansing both the grime and the troubled thoughts that had accumulated.

Aurum shouted through the partition. "I'll meet you outside!"

Sheysu finished freshening up and walked outside. She looked towards the Elders' tent and felt her palms dampen apprehensively as she wondered if her misgivings about the Canidae were about to come true.

# FOOD FOR THOUGHT

Sheysu toyed nervously with the loops on her belt as they approached the Elders' tent. Cain was entering the tent carrying a large plate of food, but he didn't look at them. A delicious aroma floated in the air and her stomach rumbled in response. Aurum held open the tent for her, and upon entering, they were greeted by the loud hum of conversation. A group of men of varying ages, but mostly older, sat around a table laden with food. They were deep in conversation. When they realised Sheysu and Aurum had entered, all conversation stopped abruptly and they turned to look at them. The silence unnerved Sheysu and she didn't know where to look or what to do. Thankfully, Lupinum got up from the table and came towards them with a big welcoming smile.

"Please, come and join us. The food is hot and hopefully to your liking."

Sheysu followed Lupinum to the table where two empty chairs had been left for her and Aurum. She sat down between Aurum and Lupinum, feeling incredibly awkward, as once again she became aware that all eyes were on her. Was she being paranoid? Were they looking at both of them because of their novelty as

Aurum had said? Her gut feeling said no. They were definitely looking at her. But why?

Lupinum went round the table and introduced them to the various Elders, a few of whom Aurum had met before. Just as he was finishing, everyone stood up as an older, well-built man with a very ornate, grey headdress entered the tent. Lupinum turned to greet him and then looked at Sheysu and said, "This is our Alpha chief and my father, Lupus Canis."

The resemblance was striking.

Lupus Canis took Sheysu's hand and said, "I'm very pleased to meet you. It's not often we have visitors in these parts, and such a beautiful one at that."

He held her hand for what seemed a very long time. Sheysu blushed and smiled but then felt awkward and started pulling away. He must've realised she was uncomfortable and abruptly let go of her hand. The Alpha chief greeted Aurum with a familiar hug and Sheysu realised he also knew Aurum from before.

The chief gestured for everyone to sit down. More food was still being brought in and Sheysu looked with appreciation at the feast before her. Much of it looked unfamiliar, but the smells were irresistible. Sheysu noticed the chief had already started eating. She thought it a little strange, but then wondered if it was customary for the Alpha chief to eat first.

Lupinum gestured towards the food. "Please, everyone start eating before the food gets cold."

Sheysu looked at various dishes hesitantly, not knowing where to begin.

Lupinum took her plate. "Here, let me. I think you will be pleasantly surprised at how delicious it all is." He put a variety of food on her plate until there was room for no more. "I will explain what everything is afterwards. Just try it and see what you think."

Sheysu looked down at the unfamiliar fare. The aroma-filled steam rising from the plate was almost heady and she eagerly picked up a piece of dark meat and took a bite. That mouthful set up an insatiable chain reaction within her that travelled through her whole body; it was as if all her manners and upbringing left her. She grabbed the food and started shovelling it into her mouth as if she had never seen food before. Oblivious to those around her, she didn't stop for one second until her plate was clean. When she finished, she wiped her mouth with the back of her hand and then became acutely aware of the silence in the room. Slowly, she looked up to see that all eyes were upon her. Flushes of embarrassment turned her olive cheeks a rosy red hue.

She was at a loss as to what to say or do when suddenly Aurum, who was seated next to her, started laughing and said, "If I'd known you were that hungry, I would've caught an elephant for breakfast!"

"No, no, don't be embarrassed," said Lupinum. "It is good to see you enjoying the food. We take it as a great compliment."

The conversation began again and Sheysu slowly regained her composure. She couldn't really explain what had just happened. Eating had never been a big priority in her life. In fact, she had been left unsatisfied and uninspired after most meals at home, which were usually vegetarian with the odd chicken or fish. This had been totally different; for the first time in her life, she felt really full, and her reaction to the food had been almost primal. She turned to Lupinum.

"I've never tasted food like that. Please do tell me what it all was?"

Lupinum smiled, his eyes twinkling. "I had a sneaking suspicion you would really enjoy it. Now let me see... First of all, the dark meat was deer meat, caught fresh today. It has been tenderised and cooked with pepper and other spices. Then there was fish, again freshly caught and marinated in mustard. Lastly, there was a mix of wild berries and other fruit."

Sheysu made mental notes so that she could remember all of the food before her; she definitely wanted to eat all of it again. Lifting her plate, she loaded it with seconds, but this time she forced herself to eat slowly, even though she could have wolfed it down all over again.

She wanted to know more about Lupinum's offer of help. "You mentioned that you might be able to help us find Similia. Do you know where he is?"

"No, unfortunately not, but the Panina tribe have had good success at finding him and have developed a kind of system. They have used it to help cure the sick members of many tribes."

"The Panina tribe?"

"They are based about half a day's travel from here and have helped us on a few occasions."

"What animals are they associated with?"

"Chimpanzees. They are very agile and great tree

climbers. They have a history of using plants from the jungle medicinally and are very altruistic in nature, and often help those who are sick. There is one particular tribe member, Simione, with whom we have a strong connection. In fact, she was born in our tribe and has gone out of her way to help us in the past. I can get word to her and she may be able to come and assist you."

"I remember Aurum telling me about children being born in one tribe but belonging to another. I didn't realise you kept in touch. It would be wonderful if she could help, so please do contact her."

"I will send one of my tribesmen tonight."

Sheysu turned to look at Aurum. He was deep in conversation with the chief. His hand was on the table near hers, so close they were almost touching. She had an irresistible urge to place her hand over his, and wished all these people were gone and they were alone in the jungle again. But then she remembered Argonisa and his future with her, and the loneliness returned. Sheysu had known Aurum for such a short time, but she had never felt this way before. She sighed. This was the wrong time; she had to keep all her focus on finding Similia.

"You look sad. Were you thinking about your sister?" asked Lupinum.

"Yes," lied Sheysu.

"You were going to tell me about your sister and your connection with Planta?"

Sheysu recounted her story once again, of how she and her sister were brought up in Planta. Lupinum listened keenly to every word. Just as Sheysu was about to tell Lupinum how she and her sister were found with their mother, she had the feeling of being watched. Looking around, she saw Cain staring at her. Their eyes met, his expression of hatred confirmed. He looked away and then left the tent. Shakily, she carried on telling her story, hoping Lupinum would not notice.

"So your real mother did not survive?"

"No, unfortunately, I never got to know her."

"Did she say what had happened to her, or where she was from?"

"No, she only had a few minutes left to live when my adoptive mother found her."

"So you don't know where you're really from?"

"No, I've always thought I was different, but it's only been a few weeks since I found out my parents aren't my real parents. I would dearly love to find out my true heritage."

Lupinum became silent and looked thoughtful.

Lupus Canis stood up at the head of the table.

"It's getting late and I'm sure our guests must be tired. Cain, please take them back to their tent."

Sheysu looked round and saw that Cain had come back. It was a little odd, she thought, that they were being escorted out as no one else seemed to be going. Lupinum stood and wished them both good night. Cain was already walking out of the door and, as was becoming customary, they followed silently. The Elders' conversation continued as they left. She heard raised voices and wished she could hear what they were saying. Her sense of uneasiness grew. They were hiding something. She was sure of it. But what?

# SIMIONE

Sheysu awoke to the sound of voices coming from Aurum's side of the tent. She couldn't quite hear what was being said but, eager to be in on the conversation, she jumped out of bed, splashed water on her face and pulled on her clothes as fast as she could. Poking her head around the fabric separating the tent, she saw Aurum standing at the entrance. His back was to her and she could now hear Lupinum's voice.

"I really think she'll be able to help Sheysu find Similia quickly."

"Who'll be able to help me find Similia quickly?" piped up Sheysu, full of excitement at the prospect of good news.

Aurum turned around to face her. The warmth in his smile made her catch her breath.

"Simione," said Lupinum. "She's just arrived and will meet us at the Elders' tent. I came to bring you the good news and to take you to her."

As they started walking towards the Elders' tent, Lupinum spoke again. "Simione is visiting her birth mother at the moment. Children in the Panina tribe, like their chimpanzee counterparts, retain a very strong bond with their mothers. What's unusual in Simione's case is that her birth mother is a Canidae. Generally, children who are aligned to another tribe go to their new tribes without fuss. However, for Panina children, separation from their birth mothers is extremely traumatic, so in these instances, if at all possible, tribes maintain a greater degree of contact. Simione has been very good to us and has helped many of our sick. We are very lucky the contact has remained."

Two women emerged from the Elders' tent as they approached. One was older and wearing a dress of fabric tied from her chest to her thighs like the other Canidae women Sheysu had seen yesterday. The other woman looked very different. She was striking but not beautiful in a conventional sense, with short black hair tightly curled close to her scalp, and a flat nose with small nostrils above full, round lips. Her skin was darker and she had a slight but powerful frame with lean and long arms that were finished off with slender, elegant fingers. Her clothing was very minimal with a small band of brightly coloured fabric crisscrossed over her chest and another similar band wrapped over her pelvic area. She was talking in a very loud, animated way to the other woman, her long arms swinging around expressively. As Sheysu and the others got close, the two women became aware of their presence and stopped talking. They hugged and kissed each other and the older woman left.

Lupinum stepped forward. "Ah, Simione, let me introduce you. This is Sheysu, the reason we have asked for your help, and her companion, Aurum."

Simione stepped forward, her long arms

stretched out to take Sheysu's hands in a welcoming gesture with hands that were warm and firm. Her full lips spread out, exposing perfect, white teeth in a grinning smile, the warmth of which was reflected in her black pool-like eyes.

"Sheysu, I came as quickly as I could when I heard about your sister. I feel your pain and my heart goes out to you. Rest assured I will do all I can to help you find Similia and the cure."

Sheysu's eyes glistened with tears and a huge lump filled her throat. In a choked voice she said, "Thank you, Simione. You have no idea how much your help means to me."

Simione hugged her tight and, although she had never met this woman before, Sheysu felt comforted and reassured.

"Where do we start?" asked Sheysu.

"For every person the starting point is different. There is a misconception that Similia is hiding or difficult to find. This is simply not true. Similia leads us to the cure by a series of clues or signs."

"Clues? What kind of clues?"

"They can come in any form: a dream, a vision, a feeling, a sensation, a gesture, a sign—the list is endless. Similia will only reveal the cure when the time is right and the sick are truly ready to be cured."

"But how will I know when I have found the cure?"

"That's where I can be of help. I can guide you and bring the clues forward. The cure Similia guides the sick to can come from many different sources:

animal, mineral, plant and more. You can sometimes confirm you have the right cure because the source is often well known to produce symptoms similar to those of the afflicted. It is well known, for example, that someone accidently poisoned by belladonna can develop dilated pupils, a red face, hallucinations and so on. In other words, something that can cause similar symptoms can cure them. To find the cure, we must go on a journey together. There is a sacred place in Animalia, which I have always found to be helpful in the cure of the sick. It is a few days from here and is called the Valley of Sensation. It is a mystical place where people find a certain kind of peace and stillness and where we can often tap into Similia's energy. Clues often surface freely there. The clues will lead you to the cure, and you will know, without doubt, when you have found it. If you are ready we can leave today, but I warn you it is not a journey without danger. We have to pass through the territory of some formidable and hostile tribes."

Lupinum stepped forward. "I will come too and Cain will also join us. You will need help, especially in dealing with some of the tribes you may have to pass."

Sheysu flinched. She did not relish Cain coming on the journey. If he hated her, for whatever reason, how could he be of any help?

"That's really kind of you, Lupinum. You have been so helpful and I'm so grateful that you would give your time to come and help me. Thank you. I was just thinking, though, isn't Cain a bit young to go on such a journey, especially if it is as dangerous as

Simione says? I know I'm young, but I don't have a choice. I have to go. Isn't there an older, more experienced tribesman you could take instead?"

"Don't worry about Cain. He can handle himself. He has been trained since he was young. His instincts are good and his loyalty to the chief and me is absolute. It's settled then. The five of us will go in search of Similia. I will organise supplies and we will leave at midday."

Sheysu felt hopeful and deflated at the same time. She was over the moon about all the help she was getting, but the addition of Cain to the mix left a bad taste in her mouth.

# THE SEARCH FOR SIMILIA

At midday the five assembled in front of the Elders' tent as agreed. True to his word, Lupinum had organised supplies, and each of them was given a full bag to carry, made from the same rough fabric Sheysu had seen everywhere whilst at the village. Sheysu surveyed the four others. It seemed incredible that, just a few days ago, she had been on her own facing an impossible task, and now, here she was with a group of strangers willing to risk their lives to help her. She didn't know what she had done to deserve such help, and tears of gratitude formed, choking her with emotion.

Aurum, noticing her strained expression, came over and put his arm around her shoulders. "Are you okay?"

"Yes," she said, her tears being replaced by the thrill of being so close to him. "I was just thinking how lucky I am to have all of you."

Aurum gave her a squeeze. "It's been one hell of a journey already. I don't think luck has anything to do with it. Wherever you go, people want to help you. There's something about you. I can't put my finger on it, but it just draws people to you. You have a real strength of character, apart from the odd, very stubborn streak." He chuckled and Sheysu playfully poked her elbow into his ribs, marvelling at how Aurum could make her feel happy in the midst of all this drama. Sheysu was smiling now, but not for long, as looking round she realised Cain had been watching her exchange with Aurum. His look of contempt erased any momentary feelings of happiness. Feeling confused and frustrated, she still had no idea what his problem was and resolved to confront him during the journey and find out.

"Well, if we are all ready, let's set off," said Lupinum. "Simione, you lead the way."

The five of them started walking away from the village, deeper into the jungle. Sheysu caught up with Simione.

"You mentioned that we had to pass through the territories of some formidable tribes. What did you mean?"

"The jungle, for all intents and purposes, is carved into territories, each belonging to a different tribe. This system in Animalia allows us to coexist peacefully for the most part. Some tribes are relaxed about their tribal boundaries, and allow others relative freedom to pass through. But some tribes defend their borders to the death. One such tribe is the Leonines. Unfortunately, we have to pass through their land to get to the Valley of Sensation. For the Panina tribe it is usually not a problem as we are skilled Tree Walkers."

Sheysu looked confused.

"Like our chimpanzee counterparts, we have

developed the skills necessary in travelling above ground—jumping and swinging from one tree to the next. The Leonine tribe, which aligns itself to lions, tends not to venture too high into the trees, and that coupled with the fact they don't regard us as a threat, means they leave us alone. We will unfortunately have to pass through their tribal land on foot this time as only I can travel above ground. If we had the time, we could send word and ask for their permission. However, they do not always grant it, so it is best we just go through as quickly as we can. That is the first tribe whose territory we must pass through, but not until tomorrow, so you can sleep easy tonight. This evening when we make camp, we will discuss our tactics for getting past the Leonines."

Anxiety began to bubble in Sheysu's stomach. The Leonines sounded fearsome and she was the only one who had no fighting skills. Frustrated at her inadequacies, she wondered why they had not been taught fighting in Planta when they were younger. Resentment grew within her, but then she remembered the peaceful village life she had left behind and was thankful that violence had had no place in her childhood.

The jungle foliage was growing thick. Aurum took the lead, hacking into the vegetation as he walked to create a pathway for the others to follow. Cain stayed at the rear of the group at all times. Sheysu could feel his gaze burning holes in her back, and she shrugged off the feeling, moving closer to the front, not ready to confront him just yet. The moist heat was oppressive and droplets of sweat trickled down Sheysu's face and body. Curious to find out more about life in the Canidae tribe, she caught up with Lupinum.

"What's it like living in the jungle as a Canidae?" she asked.

"It's all I have ever known. We live as a unit like a large family, working as a team, knowing that we need all members to survive. Although we are a team, there is a distinct hierarchy. At the top is the Alpha chief, my father, and at the bottom is the Omega, Cain. Others are placed in various ranks between. Being the chief's son, I am second in command, the Beta. The power of the Alpha is not questioned for the greater good of the tribe. We share everything amongst the tribe so none go without."

"Who decides who gets to be Alpha and who gets to be Omega?"

"It is a combination of factors that go towards the final decision. Heritage is key. Chiefs often pass leadership to their eldest son or their daughter's husband. If there is a challenge from within the tribe, the current chief must face a series of tasks against the challenger, including fighting them. The Omega is also a matter of heritage, although a tribe member can also become an Omega if they have failed or brought shame on the tribe."

Sheysu wondered whether Cain was an Omega through his heritage or actions, but didn't feel it was her place to ask.

They all took turns hacking a path through the

jungle, and even Sheysu had a go, but found she was not as effective as the others and quickly relinquished the role. The sun was beginning to set, so they found a clearing to make camp for the night.

Aurum volunteered to gather firewood and Simione went with him. The others cleared the site and set about making camp. Sheysu felt slightly useless as Lupinum and Cain seemed to know exactly what they were doing and Cain's body language indicated very strongly to Sheysu that she should not interfere.

The sound of laughter travelled through the air and Sheysu turned towards its source to see a smiling Simione and Aurum returning, their arms laden with firewood. Sheysu felt intense pangs of jealousy and was taken aback by the strength of her feelings. Jealousy was an emotion she had not often felt, and never to this degree. She tried to rationalise it in her mind, but it didn't work. If anything, it got worse. What was going on? This really wasn't like her. Flushes of heat rose through her body. The heat in the atmosphere was oppressive, and the collar of her shirt felt suffocating. Her breathing became laboured and she frantically pulled at her collar, stretching it away from her neck, while at the same time gasping for breath. The jungle floor began moving and started spinning around her.

"Sheysu!" She could hear her name being called in the distance. Her eyes were heavy and she felt weak. Cool water was trickling gently onto her face and she slowly opened her eyes to see Aurum leaning over her, his expression concerned. Simione and Lupinum were just behind him looking worried too.

"What happened?" asked Sheysu, her voice was thick as if she had just woken up.

"You fainted. You gave us quite a scare. Your body was burning up, but you feel a bit cooler now. Here. Sit up slowly and drink this."

Aurum helped her to a sitting position and gave her a canteen of cool water to drink. Feeling a bit woozy and disorientated, she tried to remember what happened. She remembered seeing Aurum and Simione coming back with firewood and feeling jealous. Sheysu shook her head. That couldn't have caused her to faint, could it? It slowly dawned upon her. *This must be part of the sickness.* Panic rose up within her; she hadn't expected the symptoms to come on so strongly. What if she couldn't complete her mission? No one could know just yet, but she knew she would have to tell them soon in case she couldn't carry on. Feeling better, she tried to pull herself to a standing position, but struggled to get there.

Simione touched her forehead. "The heat appears to have passed. Very unusual. A few minutes ago, I could've sworn that you were burning up with fever."

Aurum took her bag and laid out a sleeping mat made from the familiar Canidae fabric. "Sit down over here. You should rest. Tomorrow's going to be a tough one and you need to be as fit as possible."

Sheysu was thankful and moved over to the sleeping mat, still dazed and confused. While she sat there, watching the others making a fire and preparing food, she couldn't help thinking how useless she must appear to them. By the time the food was ready,

Sheysu felt much better. The colour had come back to her cheeks and she felt steadier within herself.

They sat in a circle to eat and Simione said, "We must plan our tactics for dealing with the Leonines tomorrow if we encounter them."

"Does anyone have experience of dealing with them, their hunting and attacking methods?" asked Aurum.

"Yes," said Simione and Lupinum together.

Simione spoke first. "They are very territorial and don't like intruders. Like their lion counterparts, they hunt and patrol in groups or packs. They mostly patrol their territory during low light, from dusk to dawn. During the day, they are more likely to rest, with a minimum of patrols. For that reason, I suggest we cross their land during the day. If we are set upon, then we should make a stand, make lots of noise, show aggression, and make as if we are going to charge them. This may be enough to deter them."

Lupinum scratched his head. "Simione, I agree with what you have said on their hunting style, and that we should go during the day. However, to make a stand as you have suggested, with a show of aggression, may work amongst the Panina tribe, but will almost certainly get us killed against the Leonines. They will not capture us, as they are a destructive tribe and killing will be their sole aim. Any show of hostility will not scare them. The Leonines are a powerful tribe who ambush intruders. Their only weakness is their lack of stamina. They can only keep up fast speeds for a short period of time. We must work as a team to get the better of them. If we can outrun them, that would be our best course of action. They hunt in groups, and if we separate them, they will be less effective. The Canidae are known for their stamina, so if we are caught, myself and Cain will try and attract their attention as much as possible. We have a much better chance of outrunning them."

"Lupinum, I cannot have you and Cain taking all the risk. I will help distract them too whilst Simione takes Sheysu as far from the trouble as possible. It's my responsibility to make sure Sheysu remains in one piece to find Similia. One factor you have not taken into account is that I have weapons no Leonine is a match for. I have a spare gun you could use."

Lupinum shook his head. "We have no need for your weapons. It is not our way. Survival of the fittest is key, and without training on them, they would be next to useless to us."

Sheysu ran her fingers lightly over the gun in her belt. She was comforted by its presence but dearly hoped she would not have to use it tomorrow.

"If they attack, I will take Sheysu into the trees. She is light enough for me to carry on my back, and we can make our escape that way," said Simione.

Aurum nodded. "Good, I think we have our tactics in place. Things obviously may not go to plan, but we should all move forward and meet at the other end of the Leonine territory. Simione, you will have to describe where that is for me in case we get separated. Now, all we need is a good night's rest, for tomorrow we meet the Leonines."

# THE LEONINES

The sun had almost reached its highest position in the sky and the heat was fierce. The land of the Leonines spread out before them, a savannah, bordered on one side by the jungle. Aurum and Lupinum had decided the best route, although the longest, was to stay close to the jungle's cover at the edge of the territory. It would afford them some camouflage and an escape route.

The tall brown grass of the savannah swayed gently in the breeze. All appeared calm, and gazelle and deer roamed the grasses peacefully.

Aurum took the lead, and they made their way quickly but quietly. Sheysu was thankful her symptoms had completely passed and she felt normal again. She had slept well after Simione had insisted on giving her a head massage, which involved pulling her fingers through Sheysu's hair. She had been amazed at how relaxing it was and couldn't even remember falling asleep. As her mind wandered, she didn't see the large rock sticking out of the ground. Her foot hit the rock mid-step and she tumbled forward with a surprised shriek. Quick as a flash, Aurum caught her, his hand covering her mouth, stifling the shriek before it had finished. Everyone crouched down and stayed perfectly still. Their eyes shifted left and right, looking at each other.

Sweat trickled down their faces—the effort of keeping still getting harder with each prolonged second. Sheysu's stomach somersaulted as she waited for some unknown sound to signal they had been discovered. The sound never came, and everyone started to breathe more easily. Lupinum rose slowly and surveyed the land around them. Everything was as before. Aurum gestured for them to continue, his finger in front of his lips, stressing the need for silence.

Sheysu scolded herself for making such a silly mistake. She wasn't about to let it happen again, and she cleared her mind to focus. They carried on uneventfully like this for two hours. Now, they were approaching the riskiest part of their journey, an open savannah where they would be visible for about a quarter of a mile. A few trees were scattered about periodically, but not enough to give them continuous cover. Walking through the savannah, they risked being seen, so Aurum crouched down and then lowered himself until he could move forward on his belly. He gestured for the others to follow suit. Beyond a swaying of the grass, their progress would go unseen.

Sheysu's muscles ached quickly from the strenuous labour. She looked up and felt that, for all her effort, she had hardly moved forward at all. In the distance a lone hyena approached. The group winced as the hyena whooped loudly. As it drew closer, Lupinum detached himself from the group and crawled to intercept it. The hyena growled, baring its teeth and then pounced into the undergrowth. The long grass thrashed about wildly for what seemed an eternity, but finally there was one last whoop then a painful crack. Lupinum, breathing heavily, made his way back to the group. Sheysu breathed a sigh of relief tinged with regret, knowing an animal had been killed because of her.

The commotion over, they continued through the undergrowth. The protection of the dense jungle canopy was only thirty feet away when a sudden whooshing noise startled them. Sheysu looked in its direction to see a large spear piercing the ground a few inches from Cain's head.

"Run!" shouted Aurum. The five of them, still crouching low, ran as fast as they could to the protection of the trees. More spears sailed through the group. Adrenalin pumped through Sheysu's body; her heart beat wildly in her chest. A spear whizzed close to her ear, the vibrations sending shudders through her body. Remembering their plan from last night, she looked for Simione, but the sudden darkness of the jungle blinded her, and she slowed down. A hand grabbed hers and pulled her hard, deeper into the jungle. Sheysu looked up, her eyes focussing, to see Cain dragging her forwards. She swivelled her head from side to side, her eyes frantically searching every direction. Realising she couldn't see or hear any of the others, she didn't call out for fear the Leonines might be close by. Why had Cain decided to help her? It didn't make sense. Lupinum had said Cain's loyalty to him was absolute. Maybe that was the reason? Still, she couldn't help feeling uneasy. Having no other choice, she followed him as he led her deeper and deeper into the jungle.

# TAKEN

Sheysu thought she heard voices and tugged hard on Cain's hand to stop him. She could just make out Aurum's voice in the distance calling her. She opened her mouth to shout back, but Cain pulled her sharply towards him and covered her mouth with his hand. He held her tightly, one hand over her mouth, and the other pressing a knife hard in her back. Instinctively, she struggled against him, but the knife only pushed deeper, causing her to wince. Her mind whirled around in panic, and she tried to make sense of what was happening. She could still hear Aurum's voice in the distance, and the beginnings of a cry formed in her throat only to be stifled by another sharp dig from the knife. The hand covering her mouth snapped her head back roughly. She called Aurum's name loudly in her head over and over, willing him to hear, but his voice only grew fainter as he moved farther away. The others were gone and she had no idea what was happening. Was Cain going to kill her? Was this really how her quest was going to end? She prayed for the others to come back and find her, knowing there was no way she could overpower Cain. Aurum's voice disappeared into the distance and Cain relaxed his hold.

Cain had dragged her amongst tall bamboo, where they were caged on all sides by the thick, green stems. Perspiration dripped down her face and body and she longed for a cool breeze. The bamboo pushed them together within its narrow confines and she wriggled uncomfortably, aware of the close contact, but this only served to make him tighten his grip. Their bodies stuck together with sweat and she could smell the musty salt from his body. A curious warmth rose through her and Sheysu started to relax. Confused by what was happening, she tried to think, but her mind was hollow and distant. The warmth felt good—her skin was tingling. Inexplicably, she felt herself pushing back towards Cain, wanting to get closer. He ran his knife-holding hand down over her body. She shivered from the touch of flesh mixed with steel. The sensations spread farther, no thoughts—just feelings. Her head turned instinctively towards his and her eyes travelled upwards, following the lines of his throat. His lips were drawn tightly across his clenched jaw. As her eyes met his, she found herself looking into an expression of warmth and momentary confusion, but it was quickly replaced with contempt. An unpleasant smile formed on his lips and she heard his muffled laughter. His hand moved from her mouth to her back, and abruptly, she found herself being pushed roughly through the bamboo towards the ground.

She landed unceremoniously with a hard bump. Horror shot through her as she realised what had just happened. It filled her with disgust and made her feel dirty. Sheysu looked up at Cain, who now stood over her clearly enjoying her distress.

"Your mother was a Canidae, and somewhere in your half-breed existence, the Canidae blood still flows. What you just experienced was the urge to mate with your own kind. It's instinctive. Thoughts or morals have no place within it. The irony is that, had your mother possessed those same urges, we would not be here now."

Each word pierced her delicate frame leaving her torn and confused.

"How do you know my mother? What…. what do you mean my mother was a Canidae?" Her voice broke, the words struggling to get past the lump that had formed in her throat.

"You really have no idea, do you? No idea of the pain, the heartache and the sheer torture your mother has caused. Didn't your mother tell you who she was? It's not surprising. I can only imagine how ashamed she must've been. Your mother was the daughter of our former Alpha Canidae, our chief. She was to marry my father, who would then have become the next Alpha Canidae. Instead, she humiliated him by rejecting him and marrying a Mineralian instead as part of some strange peace pact the Animalians concocted with the Mineralians. My father was pushed out and down, and instead of becoming the Alpha Canidae, he became the Omega: the scapegoat, the untouchable, the lowest of the low. My family has had to live with that legacy ever since. It tore my father up inside, and through the years, we have all had to watch the bitterness ravage him. I've had to endure the same treatment. Everyone looks down on me as if I'm dirt and have done so for as long as I can remember. Do you have any idea what it's like to grow up like that? To know you will never amount to anything!"

"What do you want with me? I've never met you or your family and have done nothing to you. I never knew my mother. She died when I was a baby. It was only a few weeks ago I found out she even existed!"

"She's dead? It's lucky for her I never got my hands on her. Well, I won't pretend to shed a tear. You're just like your mother. I've seen the way you look at that Mineralian. It's disgusting, as if history's repeating itself, but I won't let that happen. Ever since I found out who you are, I've wanted to kill you, but then I realised that would be too easy and would serve no purpose. Instead, I want to see you suffer, suffer the way my whole family has for all these years, all because of your mother. Why should you live happily ever after with your Mineralian after what we've been through? Then it dawned on me there is a way I can make you suffer and change the life handed to me as well. Your family owes mine a huge debt. In order to repay that debt, you'll have to come back and live as a Canidae and become my wife. That way you can't have your Mineralian and it means I have another shot at being the Alpha Canidae because of your family blood line."

Sheysu recoiled as if she was being attacked by a snake. "There's no way I'm going to marry you. Never!"

"Let me put it another way. If you don't, I will kill Aurum."

"Nooooo!" It was almost a scream. "You can't. Aurum is nothing to you. He already has a bride-to-be. He doesn't want me. Killing him serves no purpose."

"You have feelings for him. It's clear for all to see, and if I'm right, those feelings prevent you from ever letting any harm come to him. Am I right?"

Sheysu lowered her head. He was right. She did have feelings for Aurum, and Cain's threats made her realise just how deep they were. The thought of anything happening to him was like a knife in her soul. She felt powerless. She wanted to run and hide somewhere, escape, just get away. But then she remembered her sister.

"What about finding Similia and helping my sister?"

"We will carry on as planned. Lupinum has chosen to help you and I cannot go against that. It will also provide us with an opportunity to show the others a relationship is growing between us. When we join the others, you'll act as if you have begun to like me and I'll do the same towards you. That way, when you come to live as a Canidae, it won't be a surprise."

The thought filled Sheysu with revulsion. There was a bitter taste in her mouth and she felt as if she would gag. She racked her brain to find a way out, and then, almost as if he were reading her mind, Cain said, "Don't get any clever ideas about getting out of this. If you say or do anything to jeopardize my plans, then know this—whatever it takes, I will kill Aurum and then you. And don't think telling Lupinum on the quiet will help you. He doesn't trust you yet, but he believes my loyalty to him is absolute. So who do you think he'll believe?"

Sheysu looked up to see eyes of pure hate gazing into her very core. In that moment she knew there was no way out and she would have to do as he said. She had to keep strong, and as much as she hated him and what he was doing to her, her focus had to remain on her sister and finding Similia.

"So will you do what I have said?" asked Cain.

"What choice do I have?"

"Good, I'm glad you can see sense. We can join the others now. Remember, not a word to anyone." He stroked the sharp blade of his knife as he spoke, sending a shiver through Sheysu. She had no doubt he would carry out his threats in full.

"The others can't be far. I'll look for their trail. Let's go," said Cain.

Sheysu stood up, still feeling disorientated, not only physically but emotionally as well. Like a boat being battered by rough seas, she felt totally out of control with no say in her destination. She followed Cain blindly, her vision obscured by the waves of tears falling down her cheeks.

It wasn't long before Cain picked up the trail. By looking at the ground and listening carefully, he could tell the rest of the group were all together and not too far away. After only a few moments, Sheysu's heart missed a beat as Aurum's voice echoed in the breeze.

She started running, only to be yanked back sharply by Cain, who whispered a menacing, "Remember," in her ear.

She pulled free and ran as fast as she could.

Sheysu caught a glimpse of Aurum's white tunic through the trees. Hearing her footsteps, Aurum turned around and she almost bulldozed him again as she ran into his welcoming hug. He wrapped his arms around her, and she felt as if she'd come home, safe once more.

Aurum stroked her hair. "Thank God you're okay. I was so worried. I'm not going to let you out of my sight again." She wished it could be true.

The hairs on the back of her neck stood up and she could feel Cain's burning gaze. Awkwardly, she pushed herself out of Aurum's arms and stepped back.

Cain stepped forward and nonchalantly put one arm around Sheysu's shoulders.

"It was lucky she was so close to me when the Leonines struck. I was able to get her away safely."

"Thank you, Cain. I am indebted to you," said Aurum.

Sheysu looked down, hating the fact Aurum was thanking Cain and wishing she could say something. Moving forward slightly, she tried to shrug Cain's arm off her shoulders, but instead, she achieved the opposite effect of him pulling her closer and digging his fingers in more firmly. She winced.

"Are you okay, Sheysu? Are you hurt?" asked Aurum, looking at her with concern. She was unaware of her tear-stained face and the obvious look of pain.

"Sheysu's fine, aren't you?" The question from Cain was a veiled threat.

"Yes," mumbled Sheysu.

"She was obviously terrified when she thought she had lost the group, hence the tears, but then I found her and she cheered right up, didn't you?"

"Yes," Sheysu mumbled again, looking down.

"You're sure you're okay?" asked Aurum, looking somewhat confused.

Forcing a smile, Sheysu said "Yes, yes, I'm fine. I just want to get ahead and find Similia." She couldn't look Aurum in the eye, so she missed his unconvinced look.

Simione and Lupinum, hearing the voices, had now come to stand around Sheysu and Cain. Simione grabbed hold of Sheysu's hand and pulled her from under Cain's arm so she could hug her. "I'm so sorry I wasn't able to help you."

Sheysu mustered up a smile, knowing there was nothing Simione could have done, but thanking her internally for pulling her away from Cain.

"Don't be sorry. I'm fine. You've helped so much already."

Lupinum commended Cain and welcomed Sheysu back, but then quickly moved on to the subject of the next part of their journey, hoping to quickly get them back on track.

"We haven't lost much time, so we still have a couple of hours before we need to make camp for the night. We've crossed our first hurdle and escaped unscathed. Simione, what's the next one and who do we have to contend with?"

Simione looked at the group, her expression grave.

"The Arachnids."

# THE ARACHNIDS

"The Arachnids," echoed Aurum. "Yes, I've heard of them, they're also known as the Spider People if I'm not mistaken."

Simione nodded. "Yes, exactly, that's them, and like spiders, they are incredibly good at trapping their enemies. We have to be extremely vigilant as their traps are virtually impossible to see. I have been through their territory a number of times and have thankfully come through unharmed, but I cannot say the same for many others. When helping the sick and their families, I have often wrestled with the dilemma of taking them to the Valley of Sensation, versus the danger of travelling through the Arachnid territory. But when a sick person is someone close, there is no risk too great for a family, so I have made the journey many times."

After the trials of journeying through the Leonine territory and her devastating encounter with Cain, Sheysu wondered whether she could cope with the Arachnids.

"What are the Arachnids like?" asked Sheysu, her voice tinged with anxiety.

Simione looked at Sheysu, her eyes open wider than seemed possible.

"Traps are their speciality. Just like a spider, they trick you and lull you into a false sense of security and then they *pounce*. Before you know it, you're trapped. They keep no prisoners and death is quick via the venomous weapons they use. What they do with the dead is unknown, but there have been many rumours through the years. Some say they can be cannibalistic like their spider counterparts, but I wonder whether this is just a story they spread themselves to ward off strangers. The closest I got to understanding them was during The Great War, but even though we were all supposed to be working together, they still kept their tactics hidden."

"So, how do we avoid being captured?" asked Sheysu.

"Expect the unexpected is all I can say. Spiders make up for their small size by being cunning, and being cunning is definitely the speciality of the Arachnids. Each time I have been through their territory, it has been different, and I don't know of any strategy that would work consistently."

Cain moved closer to Sheysu and put his arm around her protectively.

"Don't worry. I won't let anything happen to you."

His touch repulsed her, but just as she was about to shrug his arm off, she caught the forbidding look on his face and her movements faltered. She looked round to see Aurum observing them with a confused, almost pained, expression on his face.

"We should hit Arachnid territory tomorrow

morning if we walk for a couple more hours now and then make camp," said Simione.

Subdued after their frantic escape from the Leonines, the group began walking quietly, allowing Simione the lead. Cain stayed close to Sheysu, and with much dismay, she wondered, *Was he ever going to let her go?*

# THE SILKEN WEB

They entered a clearing and Sheysu sighed with relief as the light was bright and all was clear. They had been walking in dense jungle since this morning, and it had been hard to keep their wits about them when the foliage was so thick around them. The group stood still and surveyed their surroundings.

"Everything is too quiet. Be on your guard," whispered Simione.

Just as she uttered those words, the jungle came to life. The trees began to move and the dense undergrowth rose upwards in clumps. A quiet whooshing noise came from above, and the group looked up, just in time to see a balloon of white silk descending towards them. From all sides the jungle moved quickly inwards, and Sheysu looked in bewilderment at the trees and branches advancing towards them. As the plant life closed in, she could just make out faces in the trees and leaves and realised it was actually camouflaged Animalians making the jungle move. Everything slowed down and she opened her mouth in amazement. The silken material fell fast and was now covering them. Before they could even think about running, the silk was tightened and wrapped around them by the tree imitators. They were trapped. Amazement gave way to shock and then fear. Sheysu trembled as she remembered Simione's words about the Arachnids leaving no prisoners alive and, God forbid, even eating them. Their vision was now obscured by the white cloth, but they could still make out faint shapes through the soft fabric. Aurum whispered, his voice muffled by the silk.

"Stay calm. They could've killed us there and then, so there is still hope."

As he spoke, the group was knocked hard against the ground and then rolled onto some kind of mesh. They felt themselves being lifted into the air and then swung from side to side as they were carried forwards. The silk was between and all around them. Sheysu had never seen anything like it: the sophisticated mimicry, the intense pace, the cunning, and she couldn't comprehend how it had all happened. She pushed hard against the confines of the silk with all parts of her body, but there was no give, no room for movement. It dawned on her that this is what it felt like to be trapped in a spider's web, to be cocooned in the silken web of the spider, awaiting death.

Sheysu had no idea how long they had been carried for. The group had stopped talking because each time someone had spoken they were prodded hard with some kind of spear or stick. Amazingly, the gentle swinging motion was making her eyes heavy and if she closed them, restful sleep would be just a few short moments away. But she was too afraid to sleep in case she never woke up.

The rhythmic sound of beating drums could be heard in the distance. At first Sheysu wondered if it was her heart, but gradually the beating became louder and she realised they were being swung in time with the beat. The drumming got louder and louder until it was echoing in her head and all around her. Abruptly, the swaying stopped and they were lowered to the ground. The ties imprisoning them were pushed and pulled, until one last tug and they were free. The silk fabric was lifted and Sheysu and her companions found themselves staring out into the land of the Arachnids.

In the centre was a large clearing where many adults and children, dressed in bright colours, were dancing hard and fast to the rhythmic beat of the pulsating drums. The frenzied dancing had the people in a trance-like state, oblivious to the newcomers. Around the clearing, stretching in all directions, were many large, different-shaped objects. Light glowed from inside them and Sheysu could see shadows moving within them. She realised they were homes, woven in a variety of different shapes from material similar to the silk that had entrapped them. Some were round or funnel-shaped, while others were octagonal or triangular. They were all on different levels with some on the ground or in the trees while others were on the hillsides. Between them was a network of rope bridges. At any other time Sheysu would have found the view magical, but instead she was filled with dread.

Their captors, still in camouflage, shoved them from behind with spears to get them to move.

Lupinum turned around to face them. "What do you want with us? Let me speak to whoever is in charge."

But this only resulted in him being roughly prodded and pushed to the ground. They were directed upwards onto a rope bridge. At the top was a cage-like structure, but instead of bars, it was woven out of crisscrossed cords of material. As they got closer, one of the Arachnids pulled open the strange construction and they were pushed inside. It was closed behind them, but Sheysu couldn't see how it was held together or where the closing actually joined. They all pushed and pulled at the thick cords, but there was no opening to be found. Sheysu remembered she still had a gun on her, although for what use she didn't know. She went to grab its handle, but found her belt was empty. Looking around, she saw that Lupinum's, Cain's and Aurum's weapon holders were all empty too. The Arachnids must have taken the weapons before the silk balloon had descended. She hadn't felt a thing and marvelled at their speed and light touch.

Cain spoke first. "What do we do now?" He looked deflated, and for a second Sheysu was almost happy that being caught had burst the bubble of his hideous plans.

Aurum took the lead. "We obviously need to figure out a way of escaping, but these ropes are incredibly tough, like nothing I've ever seen. We don't know what they have planned, but from Simione's description, the prospects aren't looking good. The only positive is they haven't killed us yet. Maybe, if we get to talk to one of their leaders, we can persuade them to let us go, especially if they realise our mission is compassionate. I'm determined to get Sheysu to Similia and this cage isn't going to stop me."

Sheysu welled up with tears at his words. In a choked voice she said, "Thank you, Aurum, and everyone else. I feel so guilty that you're all trapped here because of me."

Simione reached for Sheysu's hand and squeezed it gently. "No one forced me to come. I chose to and have no regrets. Don't make things worse for yourself by feeling guilty."

Sheysu as always felt reassured by Simione.

The powerful beating of the drums stopped abruptly and the peaceful silence left behind was welcome but unnerving at the same time. Three of the dancers broke away from the crowd and started walking towards them. A single loud drum beat heralded the beginning of a new drum chorus, but this time with a different, harder and more frantic rhythm. One by one the three female dancers, scantily dressed in red, blue and green, started gyrating rhythmically to the music. As they ran towards the cage, their heads swung back and forth, long hair flowing wildly around them. Their faces were heavily painted with red lips and large black eyes. Pushing their hands into the cage, they pressed their bodies shamelessly against the ropes. Sheysu stepped back quickly, her heart pounding, but then realised as she watched them reaching for Aurum, Lupinum and Cain, that they were only trying to touch the men in the group.

Instinctively, she pushed their probing hands away from Aurum. He pulled Sheysu back and the five moved towards the centre of the cage away from the prying hands. The women continued dancing, beckoning to the men, their painted faces pouting and smiling, trying to entice the men but failing.

Four men with spears walked up to the cage. The garish women moved out of the way as the men opened the cage and beckoned for the group to follow them. Two led the way and the others stayed at the rear. They were taken down another rope bridge that wound its way to a dark, shaded area. The air was cool and almost damp. Suddenly, out of the shadows, a man appeared. His glossy skin, which was black-brown in colour, reflected the little light that was present. He was of medium build and his arms were held at an odd angle as if he were about to row a boat. Something glinted in his hands and, on looking closer, Sheysu could see a sharp, curved knife strapped to each arm. On one arm she noticed his hand was missing and the knife was, in fact, a substitute. She looked back at his face, and the menacing expression together with the knives caused her to shudder.

"I am Atrax Robustus, spokesman for the Arachnids. Why have you dared to invade our territory?" He spoke very quickly but his tone was deep and aggressive, and Sheysu sensed he would not be sympathetic to their cause.

Aurum stepped forward. "We are on a peaceful quest to find Similia for Sheysu's sister who is very sick." Aurum pointed at Sheysu.

Atrax Robustus moved towards Sheysu, as if wanting to examine her, and came so close she could feel the warmth of his breath. He raised his knife-wielding arms towards her face and Sheysu hunched herself defensively, fearing he was about to strike. Seeing Sheysu's fearful pose, Aurum stepped between her and the approaching knives, pushing her out of harm's way. Anger flashed across the spokesman's face. The upward movement of his arms continued. He raised them high and then brought them down in a pincer-like movement towards Aurum's neck, his intention to kill very clear. Aurum, anticipating the strike, blocked Atrax's descending arms with his forearm, just below the knives and with his other arm punched his fist hard into his attacker's stomach. Atrax stumbled backwards from the force of the blow and clumsily tried to regain his balance. On seeing this, the four men who had brought them stepped forward, spears ready to attack. Atrax gestured to them as if to say "Stand down, I can handle this." The men moved back, standing between the rest of the group and Aurum and Atrax to prevent any interference from them.

Sheysu watched, sick with fear, as they fought. Atrax was slightly smaller than Aurum, but his lethal knives made him a formidable opponent. Having regained his balance, he continued moving forward and raised his arms up again, which had the effect of making him look bigger. He lunged forward, his knives striking downwards, aiming at Aurum's chest. Aurum ducked low to the side, avoiding one of the knives, but one caught his left shoulder, ripping through his tunic and cutting the flesh underneath. Blood seeped through the white material. Undeterred, Aurum swivelled his leg around, knocking Atrax off his feet. But Atrax was relentless. He sprung to his feet with ease and lunged forward again and again and again. Each time, Aurum found a different way to block, but Atrax kept coming.

Sheysu feared for Aurum as he was showing signs of fatigue and had already been wounded. She wished there was some way she could help him and looked round frantically for inspiration. Her gaze fell upon Cain, who was watching the altercation with something akin to a smile. Anger welled up in Sheysu and she was just about to hit him when, out of nowhere, a loud female voice shouted, "ATRAX, STOP!"

The fighting stopped abruptly and everyone looked up. There, hanging upside down from a tree high above their heads, was a woman. She was suspended by a single silk rope, which she masterfully adjusted, allowing herself to slide down smoothly whilst at the same time turning the right way up to then land on the ground without so much as a whisper. She was very tall and slim and towered over everyone there. On her head she wore a bulbous, black, glossy headdress shaped like a beehive which added to her height. Her skin was almost as dark as her hat, and the whites of her eyes and her crimson lips appeared luminous in the fading light. She wore a figure-hugging dress in the same glossy black that flared out from the knees. On her bodice was a large red emblem in the shape of an hourglass.

"Atrax, I thought we had an agreement," said the woman in black.

"Yes, but these strangers have invaded our territory and this fool"—Atrax pointed at Aurum—"has dared to get in my way and challenge me. I will kill him!"

Anger blazed in his eyes and he once again took on a fighting pose. The woman moved quickly behind Atrax. Her tall dark figure loomed over him as she bent down and wrapped her long arms around his, bringing them down. She moved her mouth close to his right ear and proceeded to whisper something whilst he was still caught in her restrictive embrace. The anger left his body like the air from a balloon and his burning expression was replaced with an almost fearful look. After looking around once more, he quickly withdrew into the shadows from where he had first come.

The mystery woman moved fast and almost glided towards Aurum.

"What is your name, golden one?" she asked. Her arm reached out towards Aurum's head and her long slender fingers uncurled one by one to touch his hair. Aurum flinched at her touch.

"Aurum."

"A Mineralian—not a common sight in these parts. You and your friends are either very brave or very foolish. Do you know what we do to intruders? We *crush* them!" Her hand closed into a tight fist, still holding some of Aurum's hair, to powerfully demonstrate her words.

"But you are far too pretty to crush. Now, that would be a waste." She laughed, the cruel ringing sound echoing in the air.

Sheysu watched the exchange, increasingly horrified as she realised this sinister woman had designs on Aurum. What agreement had this woman made with Atrax and what had she said to him to make him disappear like that? Sheysu shuddered to think. Aurum looked straight ahead and, apart from his jaw tensing periodically, his face gave no indication of his inner emotions.

The woman turned to the guards and said, "Take the others back to the web. I will take care of this one." She gestured towards Aurum.

Sheysu ran forward. "What are you going to do with him? Take me instead," she pleaded.

The woman laughed. "I'm not sure that would work. And you are....?"

"Sheysu, my name is Sheysu."

"Where are my manners? Let me introduce myself. I am Latra Mactans. You may have heard of me by my other name—The Black Widow."

Sheysu had not heard of her before, but she heard Simione's sharp intake of breath and knew the name meant trouble. Undeterred, she carried on.

"You must let us go. We mean no harm. We just have to find Similia to save my sister."

"Yes, yes. I've heard it all: compassionate mission, dying sister, and so on and so on. Sorry but that's not my problem. You should've thought about that before you trespassed into our territory. You are now our prisoners and your fate is in our hands. Maybe Aurum and I can come to some arrangement that would be beneficial to you all." The corners of her lips turned upwards into a cold, mocking smile.

"Now, guards, take them back to the web."

Sheysu persisted. "No, you cannot take Aurum. We are all together!"

"Ah, a little jealousy, some competition, that makes it so much more interesting!"

"Sheysu, all of you, go with the guards. I'll be fine," said Aurum. He looked straight into Sheysu's eyes, his expression earnest, his eyes pleading with her to go. His face became blurry as the tears welled up in her eyes. She wiped them away to take one last look at Aurum, praying it would not be her last, and then turned around to follow the guards.

# THE BLACK WIDOW

Aurum followed Latra into the shadows, where she led him to a woven structure not unlike the many they had seen when they first arrived. It was larger than most but rather dishevelled, having no formal shape, but having a very high ceiling to accommodate Latra's enormous stature. As they walked towards it, Aurum thought about overpowering this strange woman and holding her hostage, but he remembered hearing that spider people could be cold and callous. Any hostage would be seen by them as expendable and therefore, of no negotiating value.

She led him into the silken capsule. The inside was no less dishevelled than the outside. Bright red cloths hung here and there, and large, red urns were dotted around the place, covered in a white mesh-like material. The air smelt damp and musty.

"Welcome to my home. You must be tired and hungry after your journey and all that fighting with Atrax. Please sit." She gestured towards a rug on the floor with large cushions laid out at one end.

Aurum lowered himself awkwardly to the ground, sitting down with his back straight, purposefully not reclining on the many cushions. Latra opened one of the urns and took out a jug from which she poured some clear liquid into two cups. She reached up and took a basket suspended from a rope, which she then filled from another urn. Slowly, she walked back to Aurum, swaying her hips, and then leaned over him to place the cups and basket in front of him. Once seated, she handed him a cup.

"Drink this. It will restore your strength."

"What is it?" asked Aurum, suddenly worried it might contain some kind of poison.

"Don't worry it's quite safe to drink. If I'd wanted to kill you, you'd be dead already. It is dew collected this morning flavoured with honey."

Aurum took a sip. The sweet nectar tasted good and was refreshing. He gulped down the rest and put his cup back on the floor. She gestured towards the basket. Aurum looked at its unfamiliar contents.

"Fried red ants. Try some. They are very tasty, my personal favourite."

"I'll pass if that's okay. I'm not really hungry."

Latra laughed. "Not to your taste? I will get some fruit brought over."

She got up and went to the entrance and shouted out instructions to the guards who must have been nearby.

On her way back, she pulled a jug from another urn and poured some more liquid into a cup and handed it to Aurum.

"Drink, it will help you to relax. It is wine made from the sap of nearby palm trees."

Aurum raised the cup to his nose. It smelled

sweet. He took a sip so as not to offend, and the warmth spread from his mouth down his throat. Not wanting his senses to be affected, he refrained from drinking the wine and pretended to take a sip now and again.

Latra sat down again, but this time much closer. Aurum shifted uncomfortably in his seat, trying to lean away from her, but she moved one of her long arms across him, so it rested on his thigh. He could feel her hand through his trousers, and was surprised at how cold it was.

"What will you do with the others?" asked Aurum.

"Well, that rather depends on you. I haven't seen a Mineralian since The Great War. We get so few visitors here, as you can imagine. The arrival of your group has caused quite a stir. How can I put this without appearing indelicate? You are very different from the men here."

She leant even closer, and her other hand came up to stroke his cheek. Her fingertips were like slithers of cold marble and her touch made him shudder inwardly. She whispered into his ear, "If you were to stay here with me for some time, I don't mean forever, then perhaps, I could see my way to letting your friends go. What do you think?"

Aurum didn't trust her and, more than that, the idea of having any kind of relationship with this woman repulsed him. Arachnids were known for their scheming and trickery. He had heard about The Black Widow before, something about killing her mate when she had no more use for him. Even if he agreed to stay with her to save the others, he had no doubt she would have them killed as they left, and that he would soon join them.

Finding Similia was his priority. He couldn't let Sheysu down; he couldn't fail. Somehow he had to escape and rescue the others. It was his responsibility. Aurum racked his brain, but no easy solution was forthcoming. He needed more time, so he had to stall Latra.

"I'll stay with you in exchange for freeing the others as you have asked. But I'm so tired I can't think straight. This wine has gone to my head. Let me sleep for a few hours so I can tell my decision to the others with a clear head and make them understand." Aurum hoped she would believe him and give him the time he so desperately needed. Latra leant back, her expression unreadable.

"You're still bleeding. Here let me," said Latra, and before Aurum knew what was happening, she bent towards the deep cut on his shoulder and proceeded to kiss it firmly with her ice-cold lips. His wound stung from her frozen mouth. He pulled himself away, repulsed, not understanding what she was doing.

"Have you never heard the phrase 'kiss it better'?" She laughed. "You, golden one, are trying to deceive the queen of deception. You need more time you say. Yes of course you do, more time to plan your escape! What do you take me for, a fool? I was hoping you would stay willingly. Many a man would jump at the chance, but not you. Well, mark my words, before the hour is out, you will be begging me to let you stay."

"What do you mean?"

"My kiss was not so innocent. My lips are coated with the concentrated venom of my namesake, the black widow spider. It has been made from the venom of a hundred black widows, so is much more powerful than one bite and can easily kill a man. I am immune to it. In a minute you will start to feel the effects. In a few more, the agonising pain will begin. You will need this."

She pulled up a chain from around her neck, revealing a small bottle that had been hidden in her bodice. "This is the antidote. But there is a condition. I want to hear you begging me to let you stay. Then and only then will I give you the antidote. Forget your friends. Your deceit has cost them their lives."

Aurum felt the world closing in around him. He felt empty inside. He had failed. All he could think about was how he had let Sheysu and the others down. It was over. What good was anything now? She had already said the others were as good as dead.

Latra had moved away and was now sitting in a dark corner, watching him. The venom hadn't taken effect yet, he could still overpower her, get the antidote and then try and reach the others somehow, but he didn't have long. He started to get up, but then a guard came to the door, carrying the fruit Latra had ordered earlier.

She must have guessed what Aurum was up to

and said to the guard, "Get another guard and keep post at the entrance."

He could feel the wound on his shoulder stinging now, and a burning pain travelled from his shoulder into his chest. It had started. Pins and needles moved down his left arm.

"It has begun. You can feel it, can't you?" said Latra, laughing. "I won't tell you what's going to happen. I wouldn't want to spoil the surprise."

"Let the others go and I will stay," said Aurum.

"That's not really begging now, is it? As I said, forget your friends. Their fate is sealed."

Suddenly, there was a huge bang in the distance; a large swathe of light could be seen through the silken walls. Latra jumped up and strode to the entrance. She ordered the guards to see what was happening.

Aurum realised this was his chance. He sprang to his feet and ran towards Latra while her back was turned and leapt up to catch and restrain her from behind. Sensing his approach, she turned around quickly, knocking her long arms straight into him with a powerful force that sent him tumbling to the ground. She bent over him and pinned him down with her lengthy arms and legs. Aurum couldn't believe how strong she was. As hard as he tried, he couldn't break free from her grip. Skilfully, she turned him over onto his front without letting go, and then he felt his arms being tied with some kind of rope which was then tied to his legs.

She turned him back onto his side and said, "There, you can't go anywhere now." Latra got up and walked to the entrance and peered out into the glowing night.

The poison travelled more aggressively through his system. The site of his cut was now very swollen and painful. His chest muscles were constricting and breathing was becoming difficult. Shooting pains travelled from his chest down his arm, and the pins and needles he had experienced earlier were now replaced with a numb feeling in his left arm. Aurum was covered in sweat and felt cold and clammy.

As he lay there tied up, he thought once more of all those he had let down. Not just Sheysu, but the whole of Mineralia. How could he get back and help rescue Mineralia from the oppressive Queen Platina? He had truly failed in all senses of the word. His thoughts were interrupted by a bout of excruciating pain which squeezed his chest and sent shooting pains down his arm. He would never beg Latra, this much he knew. The pain came in progressively stronger waves, constricting pains from his chest to his abdomen and now also down his legs. He wanted to cry out in agony, but he would not give this woman the satisfaction. His breathing was heavy and laboured now, and death felt like it was close. "Death"—a fearful word to most, he thought, but strangely he felt no fear. In fact, the thought of death was a relief, a release from his shameful failure.

In his head he could see Sheysu's face, her smile filled his thoughts. His only other regret was not seeing Sheysu again. He had known this young, beautiful woman for only a brief moment really, but having death breathing next to him brought the surprise realisation that he loved her. He had never felt this way before, so it was a cruel twist of fate that only allowed him to experience it so briefly before his demise. The pain was so severe his body shook. His mind was becoming distant and he drifted in and out of consciousness. He closed his eyes.

# BACK AT THE WEB

Sheysu followed the others back to the cage Latra had called "the web." Her vision was still blurred from tears. She felt hopeless; nothing seemed to matter anymore. Everything had gone horribly wrong. All she could think of was Aurum suffering with that evil woman. They were pushed back into the cage and it was shut behind them.

Lupinum spoke first. "We must escape quickly. I don't think we have much time."

The guards were keeping watch about thirty feet away.

"Let's stand in a line facing the guards," continued Lupinum. "Cain, get behind and start to dig, maybe we can get out of this cage from underneath. It's getting dark so the guards won't be able to see us so clearly."

They did as Lupinum said, and Cain started digging quietly behind them with his hands. After a few minutes Cain exclaimed, "It's no use. The ropes are under the earth as well."

They all sat down deflated, and Cain began pushing the earth back into place with his feet.

"What now?" asked Cain.

"Our only hope is that either Aurum can strike some deal with the Black Widow"—Sheysu shuddered at the thoughts provoked by Lupinum's words—"or we wait until it's really dark, get one of the guards over and overpower him somehow and fight our way out. None of them are easy options. Either way, all we can do now is wait."

Lupinum reached out and put his hand over Sheysu's. "Sheysu, in case things go wrong, I need to tell you about your past. There's something I've been keeping from you. You may have suspected this already... Your mother was a Canidae. Her name was Aureus and she was the daughter of our last Alpha chief. Before your time, relationships between Animalia and Mineralia were very strained. Peace pacts were formed to ease the tension. One of them included arranging high-profile marriages between the two kingdoms. Your mother was originally betrothed to Cain's father, but the peace pact superseded that arrangement, and your mother then married a Mineralian, called Iodum. They were very happy by all accounts, and soon, you and your sister were born. Things began to go wrong shortly after. Iodum was found standing over the dead body of your aunt, Aureus's sister, with her blood on his hands. The murder weapon was never found. He was accused of her murder and protested his innocence vehemently, but nonetheless, he was found guilty by our Elders. The punishment for the crime was death. Iodum persisted in declaring his innocence and your mother believed him. The night before his execution, your mother helped him to escape and they both fled, together with you and your sister. Search parties were sent out and one managed to intercept them. Iodum was killed, but your mother managed to escape, and it wasn't until we came across you, that we discovered what happened to her."

Listening to the story was a surreal experience for Sheysu. She had already heard some of it from Cain, but now she was learning more about two of the most important people in her life. For the first time, she now had a name for the father she had never known, and within the same breath, she learnt about his death. Her mind told her she should be feeling so many different emotions, but inside she felt strangely empty, almost hollow. The emptiness was accompanied by a deep ache, a pain for a loss that could never be recovered; a pain for what could have been. She sighed, a deep, guttural noise, which attempted to release some of the hurt, but failed dismally in its purpose.

Simione moved closer to Sheysu and put her arm around her, hugging her close. "You poor thing. You've been through so much, and now to have to contend with this. It is really heart-breaking."

Sheysu felt completely drained of all emotion. It was as if her mind and body could take no more. The pain was still there but she felt flat. "Thank you, Simione." Her voice was dull and lifeless. "I'm not sure what the point of anything is anymore. Lupinum, I appreciate you telling me. I had suspected some of it." She stole a glance at Cain, but his eyes were pointing downwards, following the movement of his feet as he continued pushing earth around. "But I had no idea of the shocking circumstances surrounding my parents' deaths."

"You have a right to know," said Lupinum. "I had to tell you in case anything happens to us. Not that it will. We can't give up. We have to work as a team. Don't lose sight of what we are here for—to save your sister. You can both have a life back at the Canidae village, if you want it." Cain's head shot up at Lupinum's words and he looked straight at Sheysu, his eyes forbidding her to say anything. She wanted to laugh hysterically. Did Cain think he had any hopes of his twisted plans working? They were trapped, awaiting death. Was that too difficult for his warped mind to comprehend?

"Until today, my confidence had grown and I was so sure we would find Similia, but now, without Aurum and with us being trapped here like this, I feel hopeless. I can't see a way out," said Sheysu, her shoulders hunched in resignation.

Lupinum, stood up as if ready to take action. "I refuse to let these Arachnids get the better of us. I am going to be the next Alpha chief and I'm not going to let something simple like this rope cage get in my way. We will escape. There has to be a way, something obvious we haven't thought about. If we work as a team, I am sure we can get through this."

"I must have a closer look at this cage," said Simione. "I'm curious to see how it shuts. There's no obvious lock or catch to close it, so I'm going to see if

I can figure it out." Simione walked over to the cage's entrance and began examining it.

The sun had set over the Arachnids and it was becoming difficult to see in the dark. A very soft glow of light from some of the nearby silk homes gave them some visibility. Pounding beats from the drums, which had been quiet for some time, started once again with their hard, pulsating rhythms. Arachnids came out from everywhere to dance to the hypnotic sounds.

Lupinum, who had been pacing up and down the cage, stopped suddenly. "This is our chance to overpower one of the guards. The loud drums and the dark will help us to escape unnoticed. Cain, you and I will start fighting. Simione, you call the guards and shout frantically telling them to do something. Hopefully, one of them will enter and then I will overpower him. If the other guard comes too, then Cain and Simione, knock him out so we can escape."

Cain and Lupinum started to hit each other, and Simione was just positioning herself to shout out, when out of nowhere the boom of a distant, massive explosion reverberated all around them. Everyone looked up to see a vast fireball light up the night sky, just behind the dancers. Arachnids screamed and ran in all directions. The flames spread quickly along the rope bridges, and within seconds, many of the homes were alight. The guards who were keeping watch ran towards the flames to help.

"Everyone stand towards the front of the cage." A man's voice came from the shadows behind them. Sheysu turned to look and could just make out a man dressed all in black. His face was covered and all that could be seen were the whites of his eyes. He took two tubes from his pockets and made fire with the contents in the same way Aurum had. The ropes caught light around them and he pulled the burnt threads apart easily, forming an opening for them to escape through.

"Here, take your weapons and supplies. I was lucky enough to see where they put them. Go quickly. You don't have much time before the Arachnids realise," said the stranger, holding the charred ropes apart as he handed the weapons and bags to Lupinum.

The group ran quickly through the opening.

Once out of the cage Sheysu asked, "Who are you? Why are you helping us?" She turned around to hear his answer and, with dismay, realised he had already gone, disappearing into the night as quickly as he had come. There was no time to dwell on the mysterious stranger. They had to act fast.

"We have to rescue Aurum," said Sheysu.

Cain shook his head. "No, we don't have time. You heard the man. We have to make a run for it before it's too late. Think of your sister."

"No, I'm not going until we get Aurum."

"Sheysu's right," said Lupinum. "We work as a team and we stay together as a team. Let's go to the Black Widow's den."

Lupinum handed Sheysu her weapon. Sheysu took it gladly and slipped it firmly into her belt, patting it reassuringly. The Black Widow would be no match for her gun and, this time, she would have no hesitation in using it.

They ran down the rope bridge, unnoticed by the Arachnids who were all preoccupied with the fire. As they approached Latra's lair, the air was cool and damp as before. They were half expecting to see Atrax Robustus leap out of the shadows and they weren't disappointed. He jumped from the undergrowth, arms held high, ready to attack, his knives glinting as they caught the moonlight. He hurled himself towards Lupinum. Cain intercepted him mid-air and pushed him off balance. Atrax was undeterred.

"This time, Latra isn't here to save you. I'll finish the job I started," he said. With that he leapt towards them once again.

Lupinum shouted, "Simione, go find Aurum! Cain and I will deal with this one!"

Simione grabbed Sheysu's hand and pulled her around the fighting trio, leading her towards the glow of Latra's den.

They approached Latra's home cautiously. Simione whispered, "Latra's standing in the doorway. Let's go round to the side. I will charge into her and you come in after me. Make sure your gun is ready."

Sheysu reached down and quickly pulled her gun from its resting place and twisted the dial. As they slid quietly against the side of Latra's lair, Sheysu peered hard through the silk material and began to worry as there was no sign of movement inside. Simione gestured that she was going to go in and that Sheysu should follow. They ran quickly building up speed as they moved round towards the front. Latra was still in the doorway. Simione leapt into the air and took Latra by surprise, kicking both her feet forward and striking her squarely in the stomach, sending her tumbling backwards onto the floor. Without hesitation, Simione jumped on her and pounded her fists into Latra's head and body.

Sheysu was both taken aback and thankful for the aggression that gentle Simione appeared capable of. As the two fought, Sheysu needed no encouragement and ran through the doorway beside them. Her eyes searched frantically for Aurum, but she couldn't find him. Wildly, she ran around, looking everywhere, and then let out a loud sigh of relief as she caught sight of his legs sticking out from behind a cushion. She ran forward, putting her gun back in its belt, and knelt beside him. His eyes were closed and his face was pale. He looked so helpless lying there tied up. She quickly untied the ropes that bound him and then leant close to hear his breathing. No sign of life was visible and Sheysu feared the worst. She had seen the physician in Planta try to revive patients many times and began pounding his chest. There was no response so she leant forward and placed her lips against his and blew. Sheysu had visualised kissing Aurum in the last few days, but not like this. His lips were cold and his skin felt clammy. Tears streamed down her face and she pounded his chest furiously and blew into his mouth.

"Aurum, stay alive! Don't leave me!' She shouted again and again, willing for him to hear.

Sheysu carried on for what seemed an eternity, but still Aurum didn't move. *This can't be happening.* It was like a living nightmare. Feeling helpless, she looked around for support from Simione, but she was still fighting Latra. Simione was swinging around the room using the red cloths hanging from the ceiling to propel herself forwards, pounding her feet into Latra again and again from different angles. But Latra, like Atrax, was relentless and showed no signs of weakening. Maybe she could shoot Latra, but they were moving so quickly, she was afraid she might hit Simione instead.

In a last-ditch attempt to revive him, Sheysu hit Aurum's chest and put her lips against his once more. Still, he gave no sign of life. Sobbing, she collapsed onto his chest, not caring what happened to anyone anymore. Something touched her hair and she looked up expecting to see Simione, but was overjoyed to look into Aurum's half-open eyes, his hand on her hair.

He could barely keep his eyes open and whispered, "Latra poisoned me... antidote is around her neck."

With the effort of those words, he closed his eyes again. Sheysu jumped up with a new-found urgency to obtain the antidote from Latra.

Simione was sitting on top of Latra, who was trying to choke her with long bony fingers. Simione was pounding Latra's head with one hand whilst trying to remove the widow's hands from her neck with the other. Sheysu looked around for something heavy and spotted a heavy earthenware jug not far from where the two were fighting. She picked up the jug with considerable effort and proceeded to smash it down on Latra's head. Latra's arms fell abruptly from Simione's throat, and blood seeped from a large gash on her forehead. Her eyes were closed and her body lifeless. Simione got off Latra, saying, "Thanks, I don't know how much longer I could've kept fighting."

Sheysu moved around to the front of Latra, looking for the antidote. Around Latra's neck, she spotted a chain and began to pull it free, but it seemed to be caught. She tugged harder and just as a small bottle appeared from Latra's bodice, a bony hand shot up and grabbed her tightly around the wrist. She looked up to see Latra's black eyes staring at her with cold venom. Latra raised her other hand to strike Sheysu, but before she could, Sheysu grabbed the gun from her belt with her free hand and shot Latra squarely in the chest. Once again Latra's hands dropped lifelessly to the floor, and blood oozed from her chest, merging with the red hourglass emblem on her bodice. Her eyes remained open, the look of cold venom preserved for an eternity.

With no time to dwell on her first kill, Sheysu snapped the bottle from its chain and ran over to Aurum. She lifted his head gently, opened his mouth and poured in the bottle's contents. Aurum coughed and spluttered, but remained unconscious. Sheysu had no idea how long the antidote would take, or if it would even work.

Seconds later, Lupinum and Cain came running in. "Atrax won't be bothering anyone for a while," said Lupinum.

Seeing Aurum on the floor he said, "What happened?"

Sheysu explained what she knew.

"Cain and I will carry Aurum," said Lupinum. "We must make our escape quickly. I don't know how long the guards will remain occupied with the fire."

They hoisted Aurum between them and quickly ran out of Latra's den. Simione and Sheysu followed. Once outside, Simione led them up a rope bridge to a hillside that led them away from the Arachnids. They moved briskly but quietly, acutely aware they could be caught at any moment.

The jungle was pitch-black, forcing Sheysu to follow Simione very closely. Every now and then, the moon's rays spiked through the trees, helping her see. For over an hour, they walked in complete silence, just to be sure the Arachnids were no longer a threat. Aurum still hadn't come round fully but had moaned a few times, reassuring Sheysu he was still alive. When they finally stopped, Sheysu rushed over to Aurum to see how he was doing.

"I'm going to find some herbs to make a tonic to help him recover," said Simione, who then went off into the darkness before Sheysu could thank her.

Sheysu stroked Aurum's forehead, which no longer felt cold and clammy. Some of the colour had returned to his face, and his breathing was now audible and steady. Lupinum and Cain began to make camp.

After a short time, Aurum opened his eyes. He saw Sheysu and managed a weak smile.

"Aurum, thank God you're alright," said Sheysu. The relief in her voice was unmistakeable.

"Once again you've saved me when I should've been looking after you. Thank you, Sheysu." His hand reached up and cupped her cheek. She put her hand over his, holding him against her, savouring the warmth of his touch.

"Sheysu, when Latra poisoned me and I thought I was going to die, I realised what was important to me. I need to tell you that I…"

"He's awake at last!" Cain's voice came blasting out from behind them.

Sheysu instinctively dropped Aurum's hand.

"You've had a very lucky escape, Aurum!" said Cain, standing over the two of them. Sheysu kept her head lowered, unable to look Cain in the eye. She wondered what Aurum had been about to say, but Cain now sat down next to her, so any chance for privacy was gone. Cain leant over and placed an arm on Sheysu's shoulder. She shrugged in an attempt to remove it, but his arm didn't budge. Aurum was tired again and closed his eyes.

"I think Lupinum needs some help." Sheysu got up and walked over to Lupinum, who was preparing food, leaving Cain sitting awkwardly next to Aurum.

Simione came back through the trees clutching a variety of flowers, leaves, and twigs that she brought over to Sheysu, saying, "Help me crush these while I heat some water so we can make a tea. It will energise him and help him to recover more quickly."

Having helped her mother many times to make various teas from the plant-life they had collected from the forest, Sheysu knew exactly what to do. She took the various plants from Simione and looked around for a large flat stone and a smaller, heavier one. Once she had found the right stones, Sheysu laid the plants out on the larger stone and started pounding them with the smaller one. After a short while, she had a rather unappetising-looking pulp, which Simione scraped off into a piece of fine fabric she had ripped from some bedding. Simione gathered the edges of the fabric around the pulp and tied a knot to hold the pulp in place and then lowered it into a mug of hot water.

"I'll get Aurum to drink it," said Sheysu and took the mug over to him. Cain had moved away and was busying himself with sorting out makeshift beds, much to Sheysu's relief. She sat next to Aurum and eased him into a semi-sitting position. Aurum opened his eyes.

"Here drink this. It will help you."

She raised the cup to his lips and Aurum took a mouthful. His face grimaced in disgust.

"I said it will help you. I didn't say it tasted nice."

He smiled weakly and kept on drinking. Soon the cup was empty.

Simione came to sit next to them around the fire, as did Cain and Lupinum.

The delicious aroma of Canidae food, fanned by the flames, filled the night air, and Sheysu's stomach rumbled in anticipation, reminding her she hadn't eaten anything since being captured by the Arachnids.

Aurum looked more alert and Sheysu felt overjoyed to see some colour in his face.

Cain handed out the food.

"I'm sorry there isn't very much," said Lupinum, "but we are lucky to have even this, thanks to our mysterious liberator."

"Yes, who was he? He disappeared as quickly as he came," asked Simione.

"He had a hood on, making it impossible to see what he looked like. But I noticed he made fire the same way as Aurum with the same tubes and powders," said Sheysu.

"Yes, the Mineralian way. Did you see him, Aurum?" asked Lupinum.

"Who?" asked Aurum weakly.

"The man who freed us and presumably started the fire. He must be a Mineralian, but what possible motive could he have for saving us?" asked Lupinum.

"I didn't see him," said Aurum, his voice barely a whisper, "but if he made fire the way you say, then he is definitely a Mineralian. I don't like the sound of it. He could be one of Queen Platina's spies."

"Well I for one don't care who he is, as one thing's for sure, we wouldn't be here without him!" exclaimed Cain.

"Why would Queen Platina want to spy on us?" asked Simione.

"I don't know, but you can't trust her. I thought it was strange when she wanted me to help Sheysu. The only person she usually helps is herself. She's keeping an eye on us, but for what? I don't like this. We need to keep on our guard," said Aurum, his expression worried.

"You're right about one thing, Aurum. Never

trust a Mineralian, that's my motto!" said Cain as his eyes locked with Aurum's, a look of contempt clear to see.

"That's enough, Cain!" shouted Lupinum, his anger barely disguised. "We are here to work together as a team. Never forget that."

Cain got up and walked away, taking his food with him.

Aurum didn't rise to the bait and closed his eyes to rest once more.

# THE VALLEY OF SENSATION

"We are not far now," said Simione. "The Valley of Sensation should be just around the next bend."

They had all awoken early that morning to make up time after their encounter with the Arachnids. Aurum had made a miraculous recovery and was almost back to full energy. Sheysu's spirits had lifted significantly since her time in "the web" and she was now full of hope once again, but felt surprisingly anxious at the prospect of reaching their destination. Not knowing what to expect, she was almost scared this elusive place they had been through so much to get to, would not provide the answers she sought.

Simione stood to one side and gestured towards the path ahead. "You go first, Sheysu. Your real journey begins here."

Moving forward nervously, Sheysu took the lead. At the bend, the rough path in front of her widened, and as she turned the corner, the brilliant sunlight almost blinded her. It took a few seconds for her eyes to adjust, and then, what she saw made her gasp with amazement. The path came to an end at the edge of a cliff. She had no idea they were so high up. Looking down, her eyes feasted on the Valley of Sensation, which lay before her in all its mystical beauty. It was as if Mother Nature had emptied a rainbow and filled the land with all its vivid colours and more. There were pools of intense blue and indigo, fed by waterfalls cascading from the deepest green hills. Huge swathes of flowers and plants varying from orange, yellow, red to violet were richly spread out over the enchanting landscape. Sheysu was mesmerised.

Someone came to stand next to her and placed their arm around her shoulder. She was about to shrug it off, suspecting it to be Cain, but then looked sideways to see Aurum looking out over the valley by her side. The moment was as close to perfection as she had ever known. She stopped breathing for fear the next breath would somehow end it.

"Is that it? I thought it would be something amazing." Cain's words came bitterly from behind, purposefully destroying the moment.

"An unusual response," remarked Simione. "Most people are usually in awe of this view. I suspect life has not been kind to you, Cain."

"Let's just get on," said Cain, the irritation plain to see in his face.

"Simione, it's beautiful, like nothing I've ever seen. How do we get down there?" asked Sheysu, ignoring Cain's comments.

"Now that's the tricky bit. We have to climb down. If you lean over the edge and look straight down, you can see that the cliff face is fairly jagged and that, together with the vines growing here and there, will help us to get down."

Sheysu cautiously walked to the cliff's edge. She was not good with heights and almost swayed as she peered over. It was a long way down and looked terrifying.

Simione, sensing Sheysu's fear, said, "Sheysu, you can climb onto my back and I will get you down, no problem. Do you trust that you will be safe with me?"

Sheysu felt immediately better. Simione's presence had reassured her many times already and she definitely felt safe with her.

"Yes, that makes it so much easier. Thank you."

"I will go first with Sheysu. The rest of you follow my lead and the route that I take. Sheysu, climb onto my back and hold on tight. I won't let anything happen to you." Simione knelt down.

Sheysu took a deep breath. She could feel the adrenalin pumping through her system. Her mind was telling her she was a fool to even consider going down the cliff face, but her gut was telling her do it, that she'd be okay. She climbed onto Simione's back, linking her arms tightly in front, being careful not to choke her.

Simione stood up and walked to the edge of the cliff with ease, no strain apparent from the addition of Sheysu's weight. She knelt down at the cliff's edge and gingerly lowered herself over the side. The lurching movement, coupled with the sudden downward view, made Sheysu's heart pound wildly in her chest. She closed her eyes tightly and tried to concentrate on her breathing. Simione was now vertical against the cliff face. Sheysu breathed a sigh of relief, but not for long.

Within seconds, she felt Simione leap sideways and then down. Sheysu took a peek through a half-opened eye but then shut it quickly when she realised Simione was actually jumping from point to point without support! She reassured herself with the thought that Simione had done this many times before. The descent continued for some time and Sheysu had no idea how long they had been climbing down, when, without notice, she felt a heavy thud. Opening her eyes, she was pleasantly surprised to find they had already reached the bottom. She let go of Simione and stood thankfully on solid ground with slightly wobbly legs.

"Thank you, Simione. There was no way I could've gotten down without you."

"My pleasure. I'm sure you would've been able to do it had you needed to."

Sheysu looked at her doubtfully.

Wondering how the others were doing, Sheysu stepped back from the cliff face and looked up. Lupinum was nearly three quarters of the way down. Next was Cain with Aurum following behind, roughly halfway down. Their progress was much slower than Simione's.

Cain looked down at Sheysu and waved. She didn't respond. He was just at the bottom of one of the longest vines on the cliff face. Aurum had just begun climbing down the same vine, when Sheysu saw a flash of metal glint in the sunlight from where Cain was holding on. Without warning the bottom of the long vine somehow tore away from the cliff face and was now dangling in open air. Aurum was suspended perilously in mid-air, hanging onto the vine, too far from the cliff to pull himself back.

Sheysu gasped and stood watching in fear, her hand over her mouth. Simione jumped back onto the rocks and started climbing back up again.

Aurum shouted, "I'm okay. I'm okay!"

With that he climbed part way down the vine and then started swinging back and forth, building up momentum with each swing, trying to get closer to the cliff face. A couple of times he managed to grab the rock face, but his hold was not strong enough and he swung away again. After a few unsuccessful attempts, he finally managed to pull himself onto the rocks. Sheysu breathed a sigh of relief. She had literally been holding her breath the whole time. Aurum's position was very precarious, but he managed to work his way down the cliff face little by little.

Simione had come back down after seeing that Aurum was okay and Lupinum had now reached the ground too. "The vine must have broken," said Simione.

"I wonder how?" replied Sheysu, slight sarcasm in her voice.

"Yes, it's strange. Those vines are very thick," said Lupinum, looking thoughtful.

Simione turned to look at the nearby pools. "I think the others will be okay now. Let's have a look at the valley."

"I'll wait for them if you don't mind," replied Sheysu.

"No problem."

Simione and Lupinum walked off into the valley.

Cain was the first to reach the ground. He looked at Sheysu, a self-satisfied smirk on his face.

"What the hell did you do that for? I thought we had an agreement!" seethed Sheysu.

"I was just having some fun with your boyfriend. Don't worry. He was never in any real danger. I saw your touching little exchange last night and just now at the top of the cliff. This is just a little reminder that nothing has changed, and that I will have no hesitation in killing Aurum if you break our agreement."

"Don't worry. I didn't doubt it for a second. You don't need to remind me again."

"Well, show me that you mean it. Come away from the cliff now, with me, before Aurum reaches the ground."

Sheysu looked up at Aurum. He wouldn't be much longer and she so wanted to stay and greet him. Her shoulders drooped in defeat as she looked at Cain and she started walking towards him and away from Aurum. She couldn't risk another one of Cain's "little reminders" as he called them, even if it killed her to do it and hurt Aurum in the process.

A smug expression spread over Cain's face. He put his arm around her shoulders, staking his territory, and led her in the direction Lupinum and Simione had taken. Sheysu didn't look back once, not even when she thought she heard Aurum call her name.

They found Lupinum and Simione standing in a sea of red flowers overlooking one of the many pools. Simione, hearing them approach, turned around and said, "Sheysu, we have no time to lose. Come, walk with me."

Cain reluctantly let go of Sheysu and she walked towards Simione, who took her hand leading her away from the others. When they could no longer hear the others, Simione stopped and turned to look at Sheysu, her expression reassuring. "Normally it is the sick person I do this work with, but since you are so closely connected to your sister, I can work with you. Nightfall is nearly here, so we won't do too much today. Tell me everything you can about your sister's illness. What the physician called it, anything you can remember."

Sheysu proceeded to tell her about how her sister had fallen ill, her fever, the coma and everything else she could think of.

Simione pressed her for more information, such as what had happened before she got sick. Sheysu's eyes welled up as she once again recounted the story of finding out about their true parentage and the shock it caused. Simione made a connection between the shock of this stressful news and the onset of Kora's illness. Something Sheysu had not considered before. They continued talking for some time.

As the sun lowered, Sheysu felt almost lightheaded. Talking about all the painful things that had happened was a great release. The sun was setting to her right and the moon appeared luminous and large to her left. It was a magical scene with the calming sound of water tumbling into the nearby pool. Sheysu realised this was the first time she had felt really relaxed since before her sister became sick. She breathed in the fragrant night air and felt a sense of peace unwind through her.

"It's getting late. Let's finish for today and go and find the others," said Simione.

"I just want to sit here for a while longer. I'll be along soon," said Sheysu.

"Okay, see you in a while." Simione left her and walked back to the others.

It was getting dark and Sheysu was alone, but she felt no fear with the peaceful energy of the valley pervading her every pore.

She didn't know how long she had been sitting there when she heard a rustle behind her. Looking round, she saw Aurum coming from the bushes, his golden hair almost silver in the moonlight.

"I thought I'd find you here. How are things going with Simione?"

"This place is amazing. Simione has started working with me, but says we'll do more tomorrow."

Aurum came to sit down beside her, placing his hand on her crossed thigh and looked up at the night sky. *Another perfect moment to hold in my memory*, thought Sheysu.

He turned towards her and said, "I've wanted to talk to you since we left the Arachnids, but somehow there hasn't been a single moment where we've been alone together."

Sheysu had an inkling of what he was about to say, and her heart sang at the thought of what it might be. The momentary pleasure was stifled quickly when the threatening image of Cain crossed her mind. She couldn't risk Aurum being hurt by Cain, so she had to do something. Before Aurum could say anything, Sheysu opened her mouth and started speaking, her half-thought ideas tumbling out.

"When you were held captive by Latra, Lupinum told me about my heritage. My mother was a Canidae apparently. It explains so much that was missing from my life. She was the then Alpha chief's daughter and was supposed to marry Cain's father, but she married a Mineralian instead as part of a peace pact. My mother died escaping with my sister and me after our father was accused of murder and killed."

"I had no idea. Well, that explains why Cain hates Mineralians," said Aurum, visibly shocked.

"Lupinum has said my sister and I can go back and live in the Canidae Village. It's our birthright. I think I would like to. Animalia feels like home and what's made it more right is that"—Sheysu swallowed before continuing—"Cain and I have developed feelings for each other and he has asked me to marry him. I know it's really fast, but it just feels right and it also means he gets a chance to become the Alpha chief." She hurried through her last words and looked down, unable to look at the pained expression on Aurum's face.

"You hardly know him. You're too young to know what you're doing! Too much has happened to you too fast. He's manipulating you to become chief. Can't you see that?"

"No, Aurum, that's not true. We have real

feelings for each other and it's what I want. Please don't tell the others, particularly Lupinum, as he might not like the idea that Cain could challenge his right to be the next chief."

"There's something else you're not telling me. I can see it in your face."

"No, Aurum, you're wrong. Thank you for your concern, but I'm old enough to make my own decisions. Anyway, you have your own problems with Mineralia to think about and a wedding and a new life to get back to." She hesitated. "What was it you wanted to talk to me about?" As she said those words, Sheysu felt her throat closing from the massive lump that was forming, and she fought back the tears threatening to cascade out like the waterfall next to them.

"No, it was nothing really," said Aurum as he stood up, suddenly looking awkward. "I just wanted to see that you were okay, which you obviously are, and to say how glad I am that a cure for your sister is within sight. Don't worry. Your secret is safe with me if you're sure that's what you want. It's late and it's been an exhausting day. I'll see you in the morning." Aurum turned and walked away, leaving Sheysu sobbing inwardly as her dreams left with him.

# THE HEALING

"I have a confession to make," said Sheysu looking at the ground guiltily. Simione had woken Sheysu early that morning. The sun had just begun to rise and the others were still asleep. She had led Sheysu down to the pools again to the same spot where they had been yesterday. Sheysu's thoughts flashed back to the previous evening and her heart-breaking encounter with Aurum. The lump in her throat was still there, and as much as she tried to swallow it, it just would not go.

She must have been lost in her thoughts for some time and was startled when Simione said, "A confession you were saying?"

"Yes, sorry, I've wanted to tell you but the time just hasn't been right. I have the same sickness as my sister. It is not as strong in me, but it will develop. If we don't find a cure from Similia, both my sister and I will die. I'm sorry I didn't tell you earlier, but I was afraid people wouldn't help me or wouldn't want me to go on the journey if I did."

Simione didn't say anything and Sheysu looked up to see the familiar warmth and understanding in her face.

"Don't feel bad. I understand. It all makes sense now, that funny turn you had. How are you feeling now?"

"I'm exhausted and a little hot, but otherwise okay. So far the illness hasn't affected me in the same way as my sister. It seems to come and go in attacks."

No sooner had Sheysu revealed her secret than the floodgates of her illness appeared to open. She felt hot and faint all at once, the red flowers spun wildly around her as she felt herself falling. Simione caught her just before she hit the ground and gently laid her down.

"Sheysu? Sheysu? Can you hear me? You're burning up again. Stay with me—talk to me. Tell me what is happening."

Sheysu could hear Simione's voice, but it sounded as if it was coming from far away. A massive surge of energy coursed through her body. The energy was lifting her, and she soon found herself floating above the ground. She tried hard to push back downwards, but try as she would, she kept floating. Looking down, she saw Simione bent over her body stroking her forehead.

*Am I dead? Am I a spirit?* thought Sheysu, watching her body on the ground. The thought filled her with fear and a heavy, black sense of failure. Is this what death feels like? She had always heard and imagined that death gave you a sense of release and that there was no place for fear. So how was this possible? She was still riddled with fear and guilt. She floated higher and higher and could see Animalia spreading out into the distance. Sheysu was being pulled away, and below her, she could see the orange and golden burning embers of the Arachnid homes. From above, the scene resembled a vast, glowing spider's web. She could just make out Latra's lair as it was one of the largest. There were hundreds of Arachnids surrounding it and Sheysu could only imagine what they were feeling and discussing. Her guilt increased at the thought of the destruction her quest had inflicted upon the Arachnids. She kept drifting, and soon, she recognised the open savannah of the Leonine territory they had sweated to get through. The Leonines were visible now and she could see groups of them dotted around. Were they, too, plotting their revenge against those who had trespassed? A thought occurred to Sheysu. Would they have to go back through these tribal lands to get home? There were many now who would kill them as easily as others would shake their hands. She trembled inwardly at the thought.

Her floating continued and in the distance she could just make out the glinting spires of Periodica nestled within the land of Mineralia. Soon, Queen Platina's palace was below her in all its splendour. Some unrest appeared to be taking place there too. Many people congregated outside the palace. Was that Argentum she could see addressing them? There was a throne behind him. She hadn't noticed a throne in front of the palace when she was there before. Someone was seated on the throne and Sheysu strained hard to get a closer look. She could just make out Queen Platina's raven-black hair and pale, alabaster skin. Argentum was turning around now and giving Queen Platina some kind of trophy. The audience clapped half-heartedly. Was she taking the throne permanently as Aurum had feared? Sheysu prayed this was not the case. How could her seemingly insignificant quest to save her sister's life have had so many damaging and far-reaching repercussions?

*This can't be right*, thought Sheysu. She had to tell Aurum. She couldn't be responsible for the downfall of Mineralia. But Sheysu continued on, powerless against the energy that seemed intent on taking her to a destination unknown.

Very soon the familiar landscape of Planta was below her. Sheysu now realised where the journey was taking her and felt herself lowering as she approached the welcoming sight of her family home. She was building up speed fast and feared she was going to crash through the roof, so she braced herself for the impact, but it never came. Instead, she found herself hovering above Kora, who was still unconscious. Her mother and father were in the room. Her mother, Euphorbia, was almost in the same position she had left her in, still wringing a cloth between her hands. Sheysu called out to them but they looked through her. They couldn't see her. What was this strange, invisible half-life she had become? The energy that kept her hovering above Kora suddenly released its hold and Sheysu began falling. Her arms and legs flailed as she tried to hold onto something to stop the fall, but to no avail. Images flashed all around her, visions of herself and her parents, mixed up with pictures of school and her life growing up. Sheysu soon realised these were Kora's memories. She landed with a thud onto a soft bed and looked down, recognising Kora's bedcover.

As Sheysu looked up and saw her mother and father by the bedside, she was hit with the realisation that she was in Kora's body. She tried to speak, but no words came out. Suddenly, a sense of suffocation hit her and she felt as if she was choking. Frantically, she tried to reach up with her arms to pull away the bedclothes but Kora's body would not respond. Pictures whirred through her mind, images once again from Kora's memories. Sheysu relived the day they learned their parents were not their real parents, but this time through Kora's eyes. She felt Kora's shock at the news, but on top of that feeling was a deep, raw pain at her parents' deception. Sheysu had not blamed her parents, recognising their actions were from love, so she was taken aback to feel that Kora's response had been so different.

More memories flooded through: Sheysu going to school, playing games, being hugged by her parents. The scenes were nothing out of the ordinary, but what Sheysu was unprepared for were the intense feelings of jealousy accompanying them. She had always known Kora was unhappy about the attention Sheysu received, but she had had no idea of the depth to which Kora's feelings ran. She had always thought that, as sisters and especially twins, they had been very close, and it hurt her to think Kora had been harbouring jealous feelings towards her. Sheysu couldn't believe what she was seeing and feeling: thoughts of revenge from Kora, ideas of making sure that somehow she would be better than Sheysu, more loved than Sheysu. Kora had kept her feelings so well hidden that it came as a complete shock to Sheysu. The scenes from the past kept coming, but one in particular screamed out at her. A few days before her sister became ill, Sheysu remembered Kora working for a long time on a painting no one had been allowed to see. In her mind's eye, through Kora, she could now see the almost finished painting before her. The picture on the canvas stared back at her, and a cold feeling of terror gripped her, a deathly familiar feeling. Before her was a giant painting of a snake, identical to the one she had dreamt of on her first night in Animalia.

The familiar snake stared back at her with dark eyes set deeply within its triangular head. Its mouth was open wide with sharp, protruding fangs, ready to bite, and a forked tongue that darted out. She shook, remembering her terrifying nightmare.

How could she have dreamt of the same snake Kora had painted? What did this mean? Flashes of different memories and information like large jigsaw pieces started falling into place. Simione's words drifted back from her memory. *"The cure Similia guides the sick to can come from many different sources: animal, mineral, plant and more."* Could this be it? Could this snake or this vision of a snake be the cure? Simione's earlier words about clues echoed in her head. *'They can come in any form, a dream, a vision, a feeling, a sensation, a gesture, a sign, the list is endless. The clues will lead you to the cure, and you will know, without doubt, when you have found it."*

This was it! Sheysu's heart leapt. This was the cure. Somehow she was being guided by Similia. She just knew with every fibre of her being that this was right. There was no doubt as Simione had said. How could she get this information back to Simione? She was trapped in this strange half-life. A coolness spread over her forehead and face like trickles of cold water, it refreshed her and she felt herself rising from Kora's body. She started describing the snake over and over in her mind in the hope that somehow the message was getting through to Simione.

# BACK AT THE VALLEY

Simione rushed to the pool to bring some cool water to bathe Sheysu's head. The others didn't know what had happened yet. Sheysu had reached a critical stage. Somehow, Simione had to get through to her, otherwise all would be lost. This was no time to panic. Simione took a deep breath and her confidence rose with the memories of her past experiences and the reassurance of the valley. She had been in this situation many times before. So often the sick were clutching to the last remnants of hope and life by the time they reached the valley, but Simione never ceased to be amazed at how the knowledge needed surfaced with the energy of the valley around them. She had confidence in this process. Everything she needed to know to help the sick was already within them. She was just a guide who helped to bring the cure out from inside them. Sometimes the cure was as simple as a thought, a change in beliefs; other times it was medicinal, derived from a plant, animal, mineral or some other substance, or a combination of them all. The valley and the process just helped to bring out knowledge of the cure. The process could be a longwinded and tortuous one that took time, and at other times, it was miraculously fast. Mostly, the sick were unaware the key to their cure was already within them and, even if they did know, they were unsure how to access it.

It was Simione's job to be a detective now, but it wasn't going to be easy with Sheysu being unconscious. She continued bathing Sheysu's head, hoping the cool water would bring her back to consciousness.

"Sheysu, can you hear me?"

Sheysu was mumbling and Simione got closer to hear.

"Kora's here. We are together."

*The fever has made her delirious,* thought Simione. As Sheysu spoke, her hands clutched her shirt collar, trying to open it, but the effort was too much and her hands fell limply to the floor. Simione pulled open the buttons around her neck and chest, guessing that was what Sheysu had been trying to do. She went to bathe Sheysu's forehead again and was dismayed to see that her lips had turned an almost bluish colour. Sheysu was sicker than she thought.

"Simione, where is Shey—?" Simione heard Aurum's words cut off abruptly and looked up to see Aurum rushing over to kneel down beside her, his face mapped with worry.

"What happened?"

"Sheysu told me she is suffering from the same illness as her sister, and seconds after, she practically fainted in my arms. She's not looking too good. Help me move her deeper into the valley to the next pool.

Sometimes the water from the different pools can have an energising effect. We have no time to lose."

Simione went to pick up Sheysu's legs, but instead, Aurum just scooped Sheysu up in his arms and said, "Lead the way."

Simione took them through some trees that opened out onto another pool of water with a small waterfall. The pool was surrounded by clusters of vivid orange flowers and the air was tinged with the scent of sweet citrus. Simione gestured to Aurum to lay Sheysu down next to the edge of the pool. She collected water in her drinking canteen and poured it gently over Sheysu's forehead. Sheysu moved her head from side to side and moaned. Her expression became frightened and her eyes moved rapidly under her eyelids. She mumbled again and Simione leant closer to hear.

Her words didn't make any sense, but one word she could make out, repeated over and over, was "snake."

"Snake... Sheysu, tell me about the snake." Simione sprinkled more water on her forehead and face as well.

Sheysu kept mumbling, but again, only a few words were clear. "Black diamonds," "brown," "triangle," "fangs."

"Does it make any sense to you? Is any of it useful?" asked Aurum.

"I'm not sure, but it sounds like she's trying to describe a snake, perhaps a venomous one. The triangle she mentions could refer to the shape of the snake's head. It's mostly venomous snakes that have triangular heads. The only one I know that has a brown body with black markings that are often diamond shaped is the Bushmaster snake."

"Why would she be describing a snake?"

"In her current unconscious state, her subconscious or Similia could be directing her towards a cure. I've seen it before. People start saying nonsensical things, describe sensations or plants or animals that end up being the cure. Look at her now. Her arms and legs look swollen and her breathing is fast. Her lips are blue and she's been pulling at her throat as if she's suffocated or constricted. It's all the kinds of symptoms you expect when someone has been bitten by a snake."

Aurum shook his head in disbelief. "She's delirious. She doesn't know what she's saying and she hasn't been bitten by a snake."

"Yes, I know, but her symptoms are very similar, and the cure Similia provides works on the idea that symptoms can be cured by something that can cause similar symptoms. In Sheysu's case, her symptoms are almost the same as those caused by snake venom. Trust me, Aurum. I've seen this kind of thing many times before. People are often guided by Similia in his many forms in their dreams or, in her case, in her unconscious state. It's part of the process, especially here in the valley and it often leads to the cure."

"What you've said rings a bell. I remember you said something like that before. Okay, I trust you. So what do we do now?"

"We need to get that snake, or at least some venom from it to make a diluted remedy that's not poisonous and will then work like an antidote. It's going to be hard to find a Bushmaster snake. The only place I know that will definitely have one is the Land of Ophidia. It's half a day from here."

"Ophidia? I've heard of it before."

"Yes, their reputation always precedes them. It's the land of the serpent or snake people."

"Don't tell me. Let me guess—they're a really friendly bunch who are just going to hand over the snake and wish us well."

Simione's lips formed a half smile. "You've guessed right! No one said this was going to be easy. Let's find the others so we can decide how we are going to tackle this."

Aurum picked up Sheysu once more and they headed back to the others.

They found Lupinum and Cain stoking the fire and making breakfast.

Cain dropped the spoon he was holding and rushed over to them. Simione was surprised at the panicked look of concern on Cain's face. So far he had expressed very little other than bitterness and contempt.

"What happened to Sheysu?" asked Cain anxiously.

Aurum pushed past him roughly, taking Sheysu to lay her down gently on some bedding, leaving Simione to explain what had happened and the link with her sister's illness.

"She's going to be okay though, isn't she?" asked Cain, looking visibly upset.

*So the boy does have a heart after all,* thought Simione. She had thought there was something funny about Cain's relationship with Sheysu, but she had never imagined he had strong feelings for her. Having seen how Sheysu and Aurum looked at each other, this was going to make for an interesting journey.

"Honestly, I don't know," said Simione. "Her attacks haven't lasted this long before, so hopefully she'll recover soon, but that won't be the end of it. The bouts are becoming more powerful, so we don't have much time. In this last one, I think she was being directed by Similia. She kept trying to describe a snake, so our best chance of saving her and her sister is to go to Ophidia and get some venom from the Bushmaster snake she described."

"How do you know it's the cure? That it's going to work?" Cain tapped his fingers nervously against his leg.

"I don't... not for sure, but I trust this process and it has never failed me yet. We don't have time to waste. We must begin our journey to Ophidia. Let's pack up camp and make a stretcher for Sheysu."

"I'll make it," volunteered Aurum.

"I'll help you," said Lupinum. "Cain, pack up camp and the food. We can eat on the move. Something tells me we are going to need all our strength to deal with the Ophidians."

# JOURNEY TO OPHIDIA

Sheysu could hear a loud rumbling in her head and felt as if she was being jostled in all directions. Her whole body ached and her eyes felt incredibly heavy. With difficulty, she tried to lift her eyelids but stopped when she heard moaning sounds. The sounds, she realised, were coming from her, but she had little control over them. Eventually, she managed to open her eyes and viewed her surroundings with blurred vision. Slowly, her eyes focussed, and when they did, she saw Simione and Cain walking in front of her, but yet facing her. It took her a little while to realise she was being pulled along on some kind of makeshift stretcher behind Lupinum and Aurum. Memories of her conversation with Simione, at the Valley of Sensation, came rushing back and then the snake... yes the snake! She had to tell Simione.

"Simione." She tried to shout, but it came out barely louder than a whisper.

Simione was quick to respond and shouted, "Wait, Sheysu's awake!"

Within seconds she was kneeling beside Sheysu with the others standing over her, their faces full of concern.

"I'm so glad you're awake. How are you feeling?" asked Simione.

"Not too great, but I have to tell you what I saw. What happened to me is a mystery, but somehow I was in my sister's head and I could see her memories and feel her thoughts. I saw a snake she had painted a few days before she got sick. It's the cure. I'm sure of it. I had a dream about the exact same snake on my first night in Animalia. When I saw it, I had this feeling. I just knew this is it. This is Similia directing me to the cure."

"I knew it," said Simione, looking up at Aurum and smiling. "You were mumbling and the word snake kept coming through. From your description, the only snake I know that matches is the Bushmaster snake. We are on our way to Ophidia, the land of the serpents, where they will definitely have one."

"You're amazing, Simione. I knew you'd get the message somehow," said Sheysu, managing to muster up a weak smile. "I always thought I would meet someone, a person, called Similia who would tell me what the cure was, even though I had heard he changes shape and form. When I had the dream I realised I was being guided to the cure, so maybe he doesn't appear for everyone, but just helps them."

Simione smiled. "Maybe he doesn't appear. Who knows? What is definite though is that it is different for everyone, but somehow each person knows when they have found the cure. Then they realise the knowledge of the cure has always been within them, but sometimes they need the journey or the process to bring it out, and searching for Similia is symbolic of that."

"That's so true. I never thought of it like that!" said Sheysu, her mind clicking as more pieces of information fitted together, slowly completing the intricate puzzle in her mind. She remembered Kora had always been interested in snakes, even as a small child, and had often imitated their movements with her hands. She had even tried to charm non-poisonous ones and make them her pets. A realisation dawned upon Sheysu.

"Simione, do you think my sister could have been an Ophidian, but born to our mother, a Canidae? She has always been fascinated by snakes," asked Sheysu, suddenly desperate for things to make sense.

"It's possible, although she wouldn't have still been with your mother when she died if that was the case, unless there had been some special circumstance. Often the cure for sick Animalians comes from their tribal animals. Sometimes it's very easy to find and there is no need to search for Similia. But within each tribe, there are many species the people are aligned to, and then it becomes more complicated finding exactly the right one, and this is where the journey is useful. On that premise, you could be an Ophidian too!"

"No!" exclaimed Lupinum. "Her scent is that of a Canidae. Although"—he hesitated—"there is some difference that I had assumed was because of her Mineralian father, but thinking about it now, it is reminiscent of an Ophidian… But it's not possible… In the ancient days, they talked of 'mixed-bloods,' those who could exist in more than one tribe, but I have never met or seen one."

As Lupinum spoke, Sheysu's mind whirred on, busily making more connections. Lupinum had mentioned her scent. It now occurred to her the strong smell, that had seemed so familiar when she first met the Canidae, was in fact her own scent too, and like the Canidae, she was also able to smell it. At home both her and her sister had always amazed their parents and friends with their ability to smell odours well before anyone else. Her sister had always been fascinated with snakes, but it had been an interest she had shared. The two of them had spent hours preparing makeshift homes for the pet snakes that Kora had adopted, much to the annoyance of their parents. Now Lupinum was mentioning "mixed-bloods." Could she really be a mix of Canidae, Ophidian and even Mineralian too?

"Lupinum. Mixed-bloods—who or what are they? Please, you have to tell me more," asked Sheysu.

"As I said, I have never met one, but the Elders have stories from the past of Animalians who exhibited the traits from more than one tribe. At birth the characteristics of only one animal were visible but, as they grew older, the traits from another animal would begin to emerge. That could explain why you were still with your mother. Historically, they were persecuted as no tribe would accept them, but then ancient writings were discovered saying that one day, more mixed-bloods would be born and that they would unite and lead Animalia. Since then many tribes have come to revere the mixed-bloods, especially in their absence, as gods."

Sheysu opened her mouth, dumbfounded. What if she and her sister were mixed-bloods? What could they possibly offer the Animalians? So far, apart from a few incidents where she had discovered skills she never knew she had, there was no indication of her having the traits of more than one tribe. If she were a mixed-blood, then the Animalians were in for a disappointment. Her stomach tightened anxiously at the prospect.

"I don't think I'm a mixed-blood. I can't feel any affinity with the Ophidians."

"I'm sure you didn't feel any particular affinity for the Canidae when you first met us. Only time will tell," said Lupinum.

"Whilst we're on the subject of Ophidians, let's stop for a while and discuss how we are going to approach them," said Aurum.

"Isn't that for the rest of us to decide since we are Animalians and obviously know more about the Ophidians than you, a Mineralian?" sneered Cain.

Aurum walked over to Cain and stood face to face with him, saying quietly, "I'm onto you. I know your little game, so don't push me!"

"Yeah, what are you going to do, wave a tube at me?" mocked Cain.

Aurum smiled coldly and leant closer to him and said very quietly, "Just try me. I dare you."

"Stop it, both of you." Sheysu attempted to shout, but her words went unheard.

Cain, his face red with anger, raised both his hands and shoved his palms hard against Aurum's chest, pushing him backwards.

Aurum raised his fist, ready to strike Cain, when Lupinum shouted, "Cain, enough! I've warned you once already. Any more of this and you will face expulsion by the chief when we return."

Cain stepped down immediately and walked off into the bushes, his body stiff with anger.

"Aurum, please accept my apologies for Cain's behaviour. Unfortunately, he holds a great deal of bitterness towards your people, blaming them entirely for his unfortunate circumstances."

"I apologise too, Lupinum. I shouldn't have risen to the bait. I overreacted," replied Aurum.

"So let's get back to the Ophidians. I have…"

Sheysu interrupted Lupinum. "Just before we talk about the Ophidians, there's something I need to tell Aurum. When I passed out, before I saw visions of the snake, I saw Mineralia from above. It looked as if Queen Platina was being given some kind of trophy by Argentum on a throne outside the palace. There was a large crowd of people there, clapping. What do you think it was for?"

Aurum sighed, his shoulders drooping. "Honestly, I don't know. It could be that Queen Platina has managed to take the throne permanently. However, she is always awarding herself some kind honour to show the people what a good job she is doing. Let's hope it's the latter. Anyhow, we can't think about that now. We have to move on and concentrate on the Ophidians."

"Okay," said Sheysu, appreciating how hard it must be for Aurum to continue, knowing that the Mineralia he loved was slowly falling away with every second he was gone.

"Yes, let's get moving," continued Lupinum. "I was about to say that the Ophidians give me a feeling of déjà vu from the time we were discussing the Arachnids."

Simione nodded. "You're right to feel that, Lupinum. Ophidians have a lot in common with the Arachnids. They can both be devious and hidden. Like the Arachnids, they hide before attacking, but unlike the Arachnids, they can spend a great deal of time plotting and planning their attacks and tactics. If you thought the Arachnid's ambush was clever, wait till you see what the Ophidians can do. I have never been through their territory, but I observed their methods in the Great War. Their cunning minds second-guess you all the way. They were able to outwit all the sophisticated technology of the Mineralians by the sheer element of surprise and their ability to predict what would happen next. Many refer to them as the terrorists of the Animalian world. They seem to come out of nowhere, and hit with such a force it is difficult for any enemy to react or recover. For them the Great War was all about revenge, revenge against the Mineralians for encroaching on their territory and killing their people. Many Animalian tribes took prisoners during the Great War, but not the Ophidians. Their sole purpose was to kill and destroy any Mineralian who crossed their path."

"I think I know what you mean," said Aurum. "When you first mentioned Ophidia, I knew it was significant, and now I know why. I remember early on in the Great War, my troop was high up on a hill. My commander sent a scouting party into the valley below. The valley had just been designated as a peace zone and we were patrolling it to make sure there were no hostiles. The men were well-equipped with firearms and other weapons. Hours went by without any sounds of a battle or struggle. Not one gunshot was heard from the valley. Only one soldier eventually returned, and that was only because they let him go to spread the word of how devastating their attack had been. I remember his vivid description.

*"We had gone in during daylight so visibility was good. We walked in formation and everything was calm. After some time there was a commotion high up in the trees around us. Animalians sometimes attack from above, so we took cover, keeping our formation tight, in the nearest group of large bushes. That's when it happened. With lightning speed I felt myself engulfed by a huge force. My whole body was constricted by something so tight it hurt to breathe. Fabric was pulled tightly over my mouth and my eyes were forced open somehow to witness the horror of my fellow soldiers being killed. Each soldier was held by an Animalian. Some were enormous and had trapped my compatriots by holding them in a vice-like grip, using a combination of their muscular arms and legs together with a crisscrossed belt-like fabric that was tightened. I realised this was how I was being held. As I watched, the life was literally squeezed out of them and their eyes became glassy with the absent look of death. The others were held by men of a smaller*

*stature. They weren't being held tightly, but they were bleeding heavily from various wounds. Their attackers' hands, I noticed, had some sharp, almost fang-like attachments, that I realised had made the various cuts that were now bleeding. I was made to watch until they were all dead. Before death, some convulsed violently, whilst others bled more profusely from their wounds and other parts of their bodies as they writhed in pain. The weapons, used to inflict the wounds, seemed to have been laced with venom. When the last man died, my constriction was released and the Animalians surrounded me. My mouth was still covered so I was unable to speak. My captor came round and stood in front of me. He towered over me and I had to crane my neck to see his face. His skin had a bluish tinge and his eyes were like black pebbles. A large tattoo of a snake covered the left side of his face, its mouth open wide around one eye. When he spoke, his voice was surprisingly quiet and his words hissed through the sentences menacingly. "Tell your fellow Mineralians what you have seen today. We have no regard for your 'peace zones.' We are the Ophidians. Tell them they are no match for us and this is what awaits them if they dare enter our land again. Before you go, I shall give you one last souvenir.*

*He took a large, black cloth bag from his shoulder and kicked me so I fell into a kneeling position. He opened the bag and laid it a few feet from me. A grey snake slithered from the cloth, its eyes the same black pebbles as my captor. Its coffin-shaped head lifted from the floor and the snake undulated towards me. The snake's mouth opened wide, revealing an inky-black interior and a tongue that darted out. My captor prodded the snake, causing it to hiss. "This is the Black Mamba, my namesake and also one of the deadliest snakes. Don't worry. It only has a little venom left, so you will have time to tell your army what has happened here today." As the snake moved closer its head rose higher and higher and then, without warning, it darted at lightning speed and struck my face. I felt a sharp piercing pain and then, just as quickly, the snake recoiled and went back into its black bag.'* The soldier only survived for a short time after he finished telling his story, but it is something that has remained etched in my mind ever since."

Sheysu shuddered at the horror held within the story. "That's dreadful, Aurum. How is that supposed to help us?"

"We need to honestly know what we are up against. To go in blindly is almost certainly a death sentence," replied Aurum.

"Aurum's right," said Lupinum. "The account, horrific as it is, is very useful. It can teach us a lot about how they attack. In this instance they used misdirection, creating a commotion, knowing the soldiers would take cover in the nearest bushes, where they cleverly waited for their chance to ambush. The soldiers didn't stand a chance. Whatever happens we must work as a team and go against our instincts to take cover if there is any type of disturbance."

"But even knowing that, how can we match their size and aggression?" asked Sheysu.

Simione took Sheysu's hand. "Sheysu, have confidence in our ability, in yourself. Look at how far we have come. Who could ever have predicted we would be here?"

*She's right*, thought Sheysu. A few short weeks ago, she would never have entertained the possibility she could come so far. Her resolve must not weaken now. They had to go on and face whatever was in store, knowing they could cope, and even better, come out unharmed with the Bushmaster snake. The world of the Ophidians suddenly didn't look as scary any more.

"As always, you're absolutely right, Simione."

"If we analyse what we know about the Ophidians, we can find solutions to their attacking styles and weapons," said Simione. "I'm sure we can develop some kind of tool against this fabric they use for constriction, either to cut it or to stop it from being tightened."

Lupinum nodded. "Yes, exactly. We need the right weapons and tools, but we must also have our tactics in place. I think the best time to make our move is after they have eaten. From what I have heard, like their snake counterparts, Ophidians are extremely sluggish after a meal, so going in then would give us an edge."

Sheysu was beginning to feel better. The energy was flowing back into her limbs. Her stomach rumbled so loudly even the others heard.

"You're hungry. That's a good sign," said Simione and fished around in her bag. "Here, I kept some food for you just in case." She handed Sheysu some bread and cold meat. Sheysu took the food thankfully and ate it appreciatively, relishing every mouthful, knowing she would need all her energy to face the Ophidians.

# THE OPHIDIANS

Sheysu had almost fully recovered. This last bout of illness had been the longest and most severe, but had now thankfully passed. She dearly hoped she would be able to get through the next ordeal without another attack. They were very close to the Ophidians now and had climbed up high onto a nearby escarpment so they could observe them from a secure and relatively hidden spot. A great deal of noise was coming from the Ophidian village. Sheysu looked through Aurum's small telescope to see what the commotion was. She could now see what Aurum and Lupinum were talking about as they had already looked at the village in detail. The noise was apparently from some sort of celebration. They were in luck, Aurum had said, as this celebration could provide just the diversion they needed. Large trays of food were laid out here and there. Occasionally, they heard screams and Sheysu pointed the telescope in their direction. Young children were having their heads shaved, but that was not the source of the shrieks. Surprisingly, it was the adults. Queues of very scantily clad adults were having some sort of blue paint applied to their bodies. The Ophidian men wore plain loin cloths and the women donned bands of fabric similar to those worn by

Simione. The screaming seemed to start after the application of the blue paint.

"What's the blue paint for?" asked Sheysu.

"We seem to have come at a very auspicious time in the Ophidian calendar," answered Simione. "Their snake counterparts shed their skin periodically, and this is seen as symbolic of a rebirth or a reawakening. To attune themselves fully to this regenerative snake ritual, the Ophidians have developed a liquid which, when applied to the skin, causes it to start peeling, a bit like being burned. The liquid happens to be blue and seeps into the skin, staining it. As you can imagine, it is extremely painful, causing some to cry out. They believe that the shedding of their skin enables them to let go of their pasts and their limitations. The paint is not applied before the age of sixteen, but to allow children to experience a taste of reawakening, they shave their heads."

Sheysu winced at the idea of burnt peeling skin. It sounded horrific.

"How long will the rituals last?" asked Sheysu.

"It can go on for a few days. Looking at all the food and the numbers of adults who are yet to be painted, I would say we have come almost at the beginning. This could really work well for us. A snake is incredibly vulnerable when it is shedding and often goes into hiding. The Ophidians will exhibit similar behaviour. The only caveat is they can be more aggressive and unpredictable if disturbed. However, even that is a good thing as it means that they will have less focus to plan and be tactical."

On the way up to the escarpment, Simione had

cut several branches from a plant. She was now smoothing down the ends of each branch with a knife.

"There, nearly done," said Simione, looking pleased with her efforts. "These branches, I think, will help prevent us from being constricted."

Sheysu took a closer look. The branches had several thorns on one side going all the way up. Before Simione could say anything, Sheysu touched one of the thorns, only to pull back in sudden pain. She looked down at her finger to see it was already bleeding.

"Sorry, Sheysu," said Simione, as Sheysu sucked her finger. "I should've warned you. The reason why these branches are perfect is that each thorn is razor sharp. If you are trapped by an Ophidian, holding this branch in front of you, with the thorns facing out, should cut any restrictive fabric they use. They will also make a great weapon to strike an enemy with. You just have to be careful to hold the thorns away from you."

"These look fantastic, Simione. Thank you. Used well, these could mean the difference between life and death," said Aurum.

"Now all we need is a plan of attack," said Lupinum.

"I think I may have one," replied Aurum. "When I was watching through the telescope earlier, I noticed some black bags being taken from huts at one end of the village. The bags were then opened and snakes were taken from them. I think they keep all the snakes in those huts. That's a relief as it means we don't have to go through the village to get to the snakes. The huts are right on the edge, so I think our best plan of action is to approach them through the jungle, when it's dark and after the Ophidians have eaten. We should split into two groups so we can search more effectively. I will go with Simione, and, Lupinum, you go with Cain and Sheysu. Speed will be of the essence. We need to get in and out as quickly as possible. There doesn't appear to be anyone guarding the snakes, but that doesn't mean they are not being watched from elsewhere. I think we have to rely upon the celebrations making the Ophidians more relaxed and preoccupied than usual."

Sheysu felt a pang of disappointment at Aurum's decision to go with Simione. But then what did she expect after she had told him of her plans? He had been cool to her ever since and it pained her, but she realised it was for the best. Cain, on the other hand, had been more attentive since Sheysu had been sick, and she couldn't quite fathom his alternating moods.

"I think you've got everything covered, Aurum," said Lupinum. "They won't be expecting us, so we will have the element of surprise on our side. Just remember, though, they are experts at hiding and can magically appear from nowhere. Let's keep our backs to each other when we are near the village so we can see what's coming. As soon as one of us has found the Bushmaster snake, we should alert the other group. Simione, you make a chimpanzee calling sound and I will make a wolf howl. That way we know when to retreat."

They waited till dark before they made their descent towards the village.

Sheysu had been feeling anxious all afternoon, worried she might get sick again and also scared about being accosted by the Ophidians. Once again, she felt lacking in the necessary skills for the task at hand. As they neared the bottom of the cliff, they split up into their groups with Aurum and Simione going ahead.

Sheysu felt a strange sensation sweep through her, a feeling that she was not alone. Lupinum and Cain began to run swiftly, and to her surprise, she was able to keep up with them. She felt the same power surge through her as on her first day in Animalia and was practically gliding along the ground. Somebody whispered and she looked round to see where it was coming from, but couldn't see anything. The voice came again, but this time she could hear what was being said.

*"I will lead. Remember, when we reach the village, we must keep our backs to each other. Protecting Sheysu is our main priority."*

Sheysu looked at Lupinum and Cain but nobody was speaking or even looking at each other.

Another voice said, *"Yes, I understand."*

*Am I going mad?* thought Sheysu.

A voice replied, *"No, you're not going mad."*

Sheysu's eyes shot up to look at Lupinum and Cain. Lupinum was smiling but his lips were not moving.

The voice spoke again. *"Sheysu, this is how the Canidae communicate when we are hunting. You are hearing us in your head. You have never hunted with the Canidae before, but our blood flows through you, and all the skills you need are within you. Try it? See if you can talk to us without using your voice."*

Sheysu couldn't believe what was happening. This was amazing. What a fantastic power to have! Focussing her mind, she spoke tentatively within her head. *"Tell me what I should do to help?"*

Both Lupinum and Cain smiled. Sheysu realised she had never actually seen Cain smile and was taken aback at how warm his face could be. The first voice, she realised, belonged to Lupinum, although it was different from his speaking voice.

He said, *"Just stick close to us and don't take any unnecessary risks. If you're in any trouble, talk to us this way and we will come to you."*

Sheysu had a million and one questions to ask about her newly discovered skill. She had memories of being able to hear Kora in a similar way, but had always assumed it was because they were twins. Lupinum must have sensed her curiosity and said, *"There'll be plenty of time for questions later, but for now, we must focus."*

Sheysu quietened her hectic thoughts and followed the other two silently, still running faster than she ever had in her life.

Soon, they reached the edge of the Ophidian village near the snake huts. Simione and Aurum arrived shortly after, even though they had left before them, neither a match for the speed of the Canidae. The group crouched behind a grass bank to get a better look at the huts. No Ophidians could be seen. Sheysu hoped most of them were still congregated around the skin-shedding celebrations. There were three snake huts in all, which appeared to be fairly sizeable, room enough for even ten people to sleep in. Sheysu shuddered at the thought of how many snakes each could house.

Aurum gestured that he and Simione would take the one on the left, leaving Sheysu and the other two to take the one on the right. The group that finished first would then survey the third hut if needed. Aurum handed Sheysu a tube, which she remembered from their first day in Animalia. Shaking it would give them some light to see with.

Fear tingled through Sheysu's body and she breathed deeply to calm herself. A number of fire lamps were dotted around, casting a glow that would make them vulnerable to being seen. However, the huts had no windows, so they would be dark inside. They had no way of knowing how the snakes were being stored. Were they in cages or moving around freely? Sheysu's stomach churned at the prospect of a floor full of writhing snakes. She tried to reassure herself as she had no way of knowing what was going to greet her and had to trust she could cope with every eventuality. Her confidence resurfaced, and her group walked quietly to their hut. The door of the hut was not locked, but closed with a simple latch. Lupinum opened the latch whilst Sheysu and Cain, who had their backs to him, surveyed the area around them. He entered first, with Sheysu and Cain following. The odour of snakes was overpowering and it reminded Sheysu of her first encounter with the scent of the

Canidae; the scent here was also new, but familiar at the same time. She shook the tube in her hand and a glow of light spread through the hut allowing them to see what was there. Thankfully the snakes were in cages, but it was hard to see the snakes within them. Lupinum and Sheysu peered into the cages, one by one, looking for the elusive Bushmaster snake.

"*I can't do this!*" shouted a voice in Sheysu's head. She looked round to see Cain still standing in the doorway with an expression of absolute terror. He was sweating profusely and shaking.

Lupinum asked silently, "*What do you mean, you can't do this?*"

"*I can't even bring myself to look at these snakes! I just can't do it. I feel sick. I have to get out of here!*"

"*We'll be out of here in a minute. Just stay there and don't move!*" ordered Lupinum, the irritation in his voice clear.

Sheysu was surprised that Cain was so frightened of snakes. Why hadn't he said anything earlier? As she scanned the cages at the back of the hut, the hissing sounds from one corner became much louder. She moved closer to the noisy cage and through the hissing she heard "SSSSimiliaaaa." Was she so desperate to find the Bushmaster snake that she could now hear snakes talking to her? Peering into the dark, hissing cage, she was presented with the most welcome sight she had ever seen: a Bushmaster snake exactly as she remembered it from her dream and Kora's painting. She let out a loud sigh of relief and Lupinum came straight over. He lifted off the crate above and Sheysu gently eased out the cage holding the Bushmaster snake. While she was carefully lifting the cage, an ear-splitting scream broke the silence. She almost dropped her precious cargo and looked round hastily to see Cain staring in terror at a snake on the floor in front of him. Cain hesitated for a second, then ran out of the door, letting it bang behind him. Lupinum kicked the snake out of the way and Sheysu followed as they quickly exited the hut. She hoped no one had heard the scream and that they would be able to apprehend Cain before he made any more noise.

But it was too late. Sheysu emerged from the hut to see Cain being engulfed by an Ophidian in the way Aurum had described. In his terror Cain had dropped the thorny tool Simione had fashioned to protect them from being constricted. His face swelled and turned a mottled red as his captor squeezed him tightly with the infamous crisscrossed fabric. Lupinum was to her left, already fighting with another Ophidian who had appeared *"Help me, please. Hurry. I can't breathe."* Sheysu heard Cain's choked, frantic pleas in her head.

Cain's attacker was wrapped around him with his head hunched over so his face was hidden. Sheysu hoped he was unaware of her presence, thus giving her an advantage. She had to help Cain, but for a split second she hesitated—leaving Cain to die would end his demands on her. But she couldn't do it; her conscience would not let him die. Very gently, Sheysu put down the Bushmaster cage and moved quietly towards them when she sensed something or someone was behind her. Instinctively, she held up her thorny weapon and was just in time as, at that same moment, she felt arms and legs go around her and saw latticed fabric being pulled in front of her. The razor-sharp tool sliced through the fabric with ease. Without a second's hesitation, she repeatedly smashed the weapon down against the blue arms and thighs of her attacker, who let go instantly. Swiftly, she turned around to face her enemy, who was holding his blue and now bloody limbs and wincing in pain.

The injured Ophidian lunged forward to strike her, but she anticipated his move and sidestepped him with ease. He tried once more and again she was able to second guess his actions. Her movements were instinctive; she just knew what he was going to do next. Cain's pleas for help were fading. She had to act fast. The next time her attacker moved forward, she raised her weapon and struck it hard against his neck. Blood squirted from the puncture wounds and the massive Ophidian fell to his knees whilst clasping his neck, a look of disbelief on his face. He lurched forward and his face hit the ground with a loud thud. Sheysu couldn't quite believe she had killed him. The scene before her was surreal as if she were somehow detached from it.

Cain had stopped calling for help, and worriedly, she turned to look at him, but his eyes were now closed and his body looked limp. Lupinum was still busy fighting the other Ophidian. She ran towards the giant-like figure holding Cain and leapt up high into the air, higher than she thought was possible. During her descent, he must have sensed her approach and looked up. She struck her now-indispensable weapon down hard against his head. The injured Ophidian let go of Cain abruptly, who then slumped to the floor. The looming figure turned towards her, blood dripping down his face and weaving its way through his expression of rage. His face and neck swelled with anger and she could see a map of pulsating veins through his skin. He opened his mouth in a menacing expression, exposing teeth surrounded by inky, blue-black gums. For a brief second, Sheysu's confidence wavered. How could she fight this enormous, muscular figure of a man? But she had to. They had been through so much and, now she had the cure for her sister, she couldn't let anything stop her.

She braced herself for his attack. He pulled something from his belt. It jangled, and when he brought it into view, Sheysu gulped. It was a leather rope about a metre long, but at one end there was a metal ball. But the ball wasn't smooth and round. Instead, it was formed of many sharp blades of differing lengths, all jutting out. He swung the leather rope in large, circular motions, and she heard the whooshing sound as it built up momentum above his head. Slowly, he moved towards her and then suddenly, like a snake springing forward to attack, the deathly ball of blades shot towards her at a frightening speed. She arched her back outwards, pulling in her stomach, and the ball narrowly missed her abdomen, although one blade caught her and she grimaced in pain as it sliced through her skin.

"Sheysu, leave this one to me." She heard Aurum's voice just before he pulled her out of harm's way. "I'm sure he's the Black Mamba from the story I told you. Look at his tattoo. I owe it to my dead compatriots to avenge their honour."

Sheysu stepped back, relieved she wouldn't have to face the terrifying Ophidian, but was overwhelmingly panicked at the thought Aurum could be killed by him. Looking at his face, she now noticed the snake tattoo, its mouth open wide, engulfing one eye, just as Aurum had described. Remembering Cain, she turned around and rushed over to him. He moaned when she lifted his head onto her lap, and she breathed a sigh of relief that he was still alive. The whizzing sound of the death ball vibrated through her and she looked up to see Aurum evading its lethal blades.

"You will die today, dog!" shouted the Black Mamba at Aurum. "You have intruded upon the Ophidian Land and the penalty for this is death. You must have known this, so there will be no mercy." He continued swinging at Aurum, who so far remained unscathed.

"We are on a peaceful mission. We knew you wouldn't understand, but we had to take the risk. We need snake venom for our sick. But now I have seen you, I realise my undertaking is greater. It is my duty to avenge the lives of those Mineralians you brutally ambushed and murdered in the jungle during the Great War." Aurum dipped below the swinging ball and managed to clip his attacker on the thigh, causing him to stumble.

"Dog, I have no hesitation in killing you for trespassing, but do not accuse me of a crime I have no memory of. Not to say that I would not gladly kill any

Mineralian who crosses my path, including you, but I know nothing of these murders you speak of."

"Don't lie. You are the one they call the Black Mamba. I would recognise you anywhere." Aurum held up Simione's weapon and managed to entangle the leather rope as it swung towards him. He pulled hard and the Black Mamba fell forward, letting the leather strap go in the process. With his other hand Aurum pulled the gun from his belt and aimed it towards the Ophidian, who was now crouched on the floor.

"Stay there. Don't move," said Aurum

"Yes I am a Black Mamba, one of the two Black Mambas in my tribe."

"And I am the other!" A deep voice boomed out of nowhere as another huge Ophidian emerged from the shadows, casting a net over Aurum, knocking the gun out of his hand, and pulling him to the ground in one fell swoop.

Sheysu dropped Cain's head unceremoniously to the floor in her haste to help Aurum. But what could she do against two colossal Ophidians?

*"Sheysu, hold back. Remember, you may have Ophidian blood coursing through your veins. Let your instincts guide you."* Lupinum spoke in her head. He had managed to overpower his assailant and was now coming over to join her.

The two Black Mambas towered over a trapped Aurum. They looked almost identical, both with the same tattoo, except one was bleeding heavily from where Sheysu had injured him, and the other was older but no less intimidating.

The newly arrived Black Mamba turned to face Sheysu and Lupinum.

"We do not keep prisoners, so how would you like to die? Perhaps"—he picked up the cage containing the Bushmaster snake—"a bite from the snake you were trying to steal! Now that would be just." As he spoke, Sheysu felt a strong breeze. The older Black Mamba caught a whiff in the air and looked confused. "What do we have here?" He walked towards Sheysu to smell her more closely. "You are an Ophidian, or at least part of you is. But there's something else. What is that other awful smell?" He sniffed the air further and walked towards Lupinum. "Canidae. That's the scent. You also smell like a Canidae. A mixed-blood? But how can that be?"

As he came back to stand next to her, Sheysu remembered Aurum's horrifying description. She now looked at his pebble-black eyes and bluish-tinged skin. He raised his hand to touch her face and she stared in fascination at the almost leathery, snake-like skin covering his body—a product, no doubt, of repeated skin shedding.

He touched her face lightly like someone examining a rare object. "I have heard of your kind but always thought it was just the stuff of legends, yet here you are. There are many in my tribe who would worship you."

"Does that include you?" asked Sheysu tentatively.

Before he could answer, Cain shouted from behind them. "Both of you Ophidians move over there, by that hut, and stand with your backs to us."

He was pointing a gun at the first Black Mamba. Cain had somehow recovered and was holding the gun that had fallen near him when it had been knocked out of Aurum's hand.

The two Black Mambas reluctantly did as they were told. Meanwhile, Aurum had managed to untie himself from the net that covered him and came to stand beside Sheysu.

"Let's tie them up," said Sheysu. "I know you want justice, Aurum, but there have been too many deaths as a result of my quest to save my sister. The Ophidians do not deserve to die. They are only protecting their land, which they are entitled to do. We are the trespassers. I will have no more bloodshed on my account."

Lupinum picked up the various latticed fabrics strewn across the ground and walked over to the Black Mambas to tie them up.

"Wait," said the older Black Mamba. "You asked me if I worshipped mixed-bloods." He turned his head around to face Sheysu as he spoke. "Don't you want to hear my answer?"

"Would it make any difference?" asked Sheysu.

"Well, that depends. In a few moments, many more Ophidians will come this way, and you and your strange mix of compatriots will have no possibility of escape, and your mission will have been a failure. To answer your question, I don't worship your kind, but I am intrigued. Being able to introduce you as my find, so to speak, will increase my leadership power within the tribe, especially amongst the many who would worship you."

"We cannot stay. I do not want to stay. We have to get back now that we have a cure for my sister."

"One day is all I ask, in return for your safe passage out of our land. I give you my word. As I said before, a mixed-blood is the stuff of legends and to present you to the tribe, even for a day, would be like showing them God."

Sheysu looked at Aurum helplessly.

"I wouldn't trust him, but if what he says is true, we may have no other option," said Aurum.

"Okay, turn around and come back, but Cain, you keep your gun pointed at them and if there is even a hint of something not right, then do what you have to," said Sheysu in a resigned voice. She began to realise that every encounter seemed to have an unexpected twist or turn and exacted more and more from her.

"If my fellow Ophidians see him pointing a gun at us, they will attack first and ask questions later," insisted the older Black Mamba.

"No, I'm not falling for that," said Cain, who then picked up one of the empty, black snake bags that was on the ground and draped it over the gun. "There! Now no one will suspect anything. We may have to trust you against our better judgement, but having a gun pointed at you will make you think twice before you go back on your word."

True to the older Black Mamba's words, a group of Ophidians suddenly appeared from the shadows. Cain kept his stance casual so as not to attract attention. The group looked confused on seeing the injured Ophidians and appeared unable to decide whether or not to attack.

The older Black Mamba addressed them. "Do not be concerned. There has been a terrible misunderstanding. These unexpected visitors are my guests. Gather everyone for an emergency meeting at the Najatera."

"But, Chief Dendro, we are in the middle of the sacred Ecdisis celebrations," the first Ophidian spoke.

"Believe me, this is more important. Go now, hurry," replied Dendro, the older Black Mamba.

"As you wish," said the first Ophidian. The group turned and walked back into the shadows.

"So you're a chief. Are you the leader of your tribe? What will happen now? What is this meeting and where?" Sheysu had so many questions.

"Yes I am the Ophidian leader, Chief Dendro, and he is my son." He pointed to the injured Black Mamba. "Do not alarm yourselves. I have asked everyone to congregate at the Najatera, our shrine to the snake gods, so I can present you to them."

Sheysu was confused by the chief's requests. Something did not add up.

"I don't understand. What do you gain from showing me to your tribe for just one day?"

"I have only just become chief. I fought a bitter battle to the death with our previous chief, Naja, the Cobra warrior. I had to plot for many years before I could overthrow him. Chief Naja was strong and powerful and there was no way I could have beaten him in a one-to-one battle. I had to be clever and conceal my actions for many years. I gained the allegiance of a few strong Ophidians, and together, we attacked. The chief and his men didn't see it coming. For them the attack came out of nowhere, especially as I was his right hand man. Many were unhappy about my leadership and none more so than his two sons. They have since been gathering allies amongst the tribe, and I feel an attempted takeover is imminent. If I bring you to the tribe as my find, a treasured mixed-blood, then those defecting allies will drop their loyalty to the Cobra warrior's sons and follow me instead."

"But why would seeing a mixed-blood make them do that?"

"You have no idea of the power and influence you hold. Our ancient scriptures speak of mixed-bloods as if they are gods. Showing them you actually exist will make my tribe believe that I have access to a divine force, and that I am omnipotent!"

"But I'm not staying."

"Yes, I will tell them and you will agree that you are able to connect to me over distance, and that you have bestowed some of your powers upon me."

"And they'll believe that?" asked Sheysu sceptically.

"If you had read our ancient scriptures, then you would have no doubts. Come, let us go to the Najatera."

"I'm not leaving this behind," said Sheysu and picked up the Bushmaster cage.

Dendro nodded in agreement.

It suddenly occurred to Sheysu that she had not

seen Simione. She looked over at Lupinum and asked him silently, *"Have you seen Simione?"*

Lupinum nodded. *"Simione escaped. I saw her run from the hut she was in after Aurum had been captured. I think it is for the best. You have the cure you need. There is no sense in her being caught up in all of this."*

Sheysu felt lost. Simione had been her rock through this whole process and she couldn't believe she would just leave like that. She followed Dendro and the others, her mind preoccupied with thoughts of Simione.

# THE NAJATERA

As they walked to the Najatera, Cain caught up with Sheysu. He spoke quietly.

"Why did you save me? Letting the Ophidian kill me was the perfect way of getting rid of me."

"Whatever you think, Cain, you have helped me get this far. I don't like what you are making me do, but we wouldn't have got here without all of us. I couldn't just stand there and let one of us die when I had the power to do something."

"I don't know what to say, but thank you. I owe you a debt."

"Is it enough for me to be free of you?"

"No." He shook his head almost regretfully. "The hurt caused by your family runs too deep, and I need the chance you give me to become chief."

Sheysu sighed, realising once again that there was no way out of her agreement with Cain.

They came to a narrowing of the path between the trees, and Sheysu slowed her footsteps so Cain could walk ahead. Aurum came through to walk by her side and Sheysu still felt thrilled just to be near him. Cain turned around and passed Aurum's gun back to him. "I guess I don't need this now." Aurum nodded and took the gun as Cain carried on walking ahead.

"How are you holding up?" asked Aurum.

"I don't know. This journey has become bigger than I ever imagined."

She lowered her voice so no one else could hear.

"Now that Simione has gone, I feel lost. You brought me to Animalia, but since we met her, she has been like my guide, spiritually as well as physically. I don't understand why she would just leave like that. It doesn't make sense. She's never run away from trouble. On the contrary she has always gone out of her way to help."

"I was surprised too," said Aurum, "but we can't worry about that now. We have to keep our wits about us. I don't trust Dendro and I've got a bad feeling about this meeting."

"He appeared genuine to me, but you're right. We should stay on our guard."

They could hear many voices ahead, against a background of steady chanting. As they got closer, the voices and chanting became louder and louder. The path opened out to a large clearing with steps descending into a huge arena. The ground below them was filled with Ophidians, some standing and some sitting. The sun was rising and cast its golden rays over a sea of mottled-blue and olive-skinned Animalians. The seated ones were chanting whilst the others chattered. At the opposite end of the arena were steps leading up to a large cave. In front of it stood huge statues of different snakes, some wrapped around Ophidian figures. A large fire burned before the stone sculptures, their outlines wavering in its burning heat.

As they made their way down the steps, the congregation became aware of their presence and the chanting and talking stopped abruptly.

Sheysu felt extremely uncomfortable with all eyes focussed on them. It reminded her of the first time she entered the Canidae village. There, it had been more curiosity she had felt directed towards her, but this time, she could feel the menace behind the stares. The silence was unnerving. Dendro continued walking through the crowd, and the Ophidians parted to make a path for them. It was so quiet the echo of their footsteps rung out through the arena. He led them up the steps to the statues where he gestured for them to turn around to face the congregation and stand by his side. He began to speak, his booming voice resonating through the silent arena.

"Ophidians, hear me now. Today is a great day. One we have been waiting for all our lives. Our ancient scriptures speak of the sacred ones who will come to our land and guide us to victory over Animalia. That day has come. Behold our first mixed-blood." He pulled Sheysu out in front of him. A gasp formed amongst the crowd. "She has been waiting for the right time and that time has come now that I am chief!"

A loud cheer exploded through the crowd and arms were raised in elation.

Dendro waved his hands down, to quieten the assembly, so he could talk more.

"For the first time in our remembered history, we will suspend our Ecdisis rituals. Today we celebrate!"

The Ophidians went wild, shouting and cheering.

Dendro turned to Sheysu and said, "Do you see the effect you have? Now, can you understand my reasons for presenting you?"

"But you didn't tell them about me leaving!"

"Do not be concerned. There will be plenty of time for that during the celebrations. Let them enjoy this news first. Come, let me show you where you can refresh yourselves before the festivities."

Dendro led the group around the side of the arena to another walkway. It opened out to a clearing, in the centre of which was a large wooden hut surrounded by some smaller ones. He pointed to the large dwelling. "This is my home. You can use the two other huts," he said as he pointed at two smaller structures, "to refresh yourselves and then, please, join me back at the Najatera when you have finished."

As they walked towards the huts the Bushmaster snake, carried by Sheysu, hissed loudly in its cage. Dendro stopped and said, "Your snake is hungry. Wait here a moment." He walked into his home and emerged just a few seconds later, carrying a small, live mouse by its tail. Sheysu squirmed at the thought of what was about to happen next.

"Would you like to feed him?" asked Dendro.

Sheysu shook her head with a look of disgust. Dendro laughed. "So squeamish for one who was willing to take on the might of the Ophidians."

He took the cage and opened the latch. Without a second's hesitation, he put his hand in and pulled out the Bushmaster snake, holding it firmly by its neck, bringing it close to Sheysu's face, almost as a threat. She pulled away, her expression one of fear and revulsion. Dendro proceeded to dangle the mouse in front of the snake and let his other hand slip farther down its body. The snake hissed and opened its mouth wide before hurtling itself towards the mouse at lightning speed, engulfing the tiny creature in its huge jaws. Sheysu couldn't watch and covered her eyes to the sound of Dendro's mocking laughter.

He put the snake with its feast back into the cage. "Let us get ready for the celebrations."

Aurum picked up the cage. "Here, I'll look after it, Sheysu. You freshen up in the hut on the left and we'll meet you outside when you've finished."

The prospect of being alone was frightening, but what could she say? She walked to her hut, aiming to clean up as quickly as possible. Inside, she was taken aback by the chaotic interior that greeted her. Unlike the clean and ordered Canidae tent, the interior here was a mess. There were cloths strewn about the place and it looked as if someone had tried to tidy up half-heartedly, starting something and then moving on without finishing. There was a jug of water and a bowl. Thankfully they looked clean and the water looked fresh. She washed herself quickly as best she could, using her own clothes to dry herself instead of the scattered cloths that looked as if they had seen better days. She left the hut to find that the others had not yet come out. Intrigued to see what kind of dwelling the chief of the Ophidians inhabited, Sheysu walked over to the larger structure Dendro called home. It was a huge hut with several rooms. She peered in through one of the windows and was surprised to see opulent and well-maintained interiors. As she walked around the side, she heard Dendro's voice. He was talking to a woman, maybe his wife, thought Sheysu. She stopped out of sight, to listen.

"Dendro, your future, our future, is assured. This mixed-blood will cause the collapse of the Cobra warriors' movement. Who will want to follow them now?" The glee in the woman's voice spilt over.

"Patience, Cenchrina." Sheysu heard Dendro's voice. "First I must dispose of her compatriots and then she will be my prisoner with no way of escape. She will soon see that life will be easier if she follows my command rather than opposing it. We will poison her companions during the celebrations. Get the necessary venom and make sure there are no mistakes."

Sheysu stifled the gasp that rose up within her. Her heart pounded so loudly it was all she could hear in her head. She had to tell the others. There was no time to lose. As quietly as possible, she made her way back to the others, who were now waiting outside their hut.

Aurum took one look at Sheysu's face and said, "What's wrong?"

She lowered her voice so as not to be heard by a group of Ophidians who were now walking to Dendro's hut. "I just heard Dendro talking. They are planning to kill you all and keep me prisoner. How could I have been so stupid as to believe him, when all my instincts screamed the exact opposite? Tonight at the celebrations they are going to poison you. I don't know how. You were right, Aurum, not to trust him. We have to escape, but how?"

Before they could talk, Dendro emerged from his hut carrying a black bag. He was flanked on one side by his son, whose wounds had now been cleaned, but who looked no less menacing, and on the other side by another huge Ophidian.

"Ah, you are ready to join the celebrations. Come, let us go to the Najatera," said Dendro.

They followed Dendro in silence, acutely aware of their dangerous predicament. Their moment for escape passed as quickly as it came when many more Ophidians emerged to join them along the path to the Najatera.

The loud din of chattering voices greeted them again as they entered the arena. It occurred to Sheysu that the Ophidians were a noisy tribe, far more talkative than the previous Animalians they had encountered. Large platters of food were being carried into the arena, and fires were being lit here and there. Dendro led them back towards the snake statues, but this time he took them into the cave behind. The cool interior was refreshing. The cave was lit by many fire lamps and their glow extended to reveal a huge space within. More snake idols were dotted around. In the middle, a huge throne took centre stage. It looked newly carved, the stone being much lighter in colour than the statues around it. The seat was large, intricate designs covering the arms and legs. The throne's backrest was carved from a huge piece of stone into a large snake that rose up high into the cave. Sheysu followed the neck of the stone snake upwards, tilting her head back to see the top. She remembered Aurum's story of his fellow soldiers as there in front of her was a carving of a massive snake with a coffin-shaped head, its mouth open, revealing an inky black exterior: the Black Mamba. Sheysu realised the stone mamba was Dendro's namesake and had probably just been carved when he became chief. Dendro sat on his throne while his son and the other large Ophidian stood by his side. There were many seats in front of the throne and the remaining Ophidians, who had followed them in, sat at the back. Dendro gestured for Sheysu and the others to take a seat in the front. He addressed Sheysu.

"Before we join the celebrations, there are many Ophidian dignitaries who want to meet you, Sheysu. I have asked them to come here. Do not be alarmed. They may ask questions, smell you and even touch you. It is just curiosity. They want to make sure you are a mixed-blood. Remember, for them you are god-like."

Sheysu half-heartedly nodded her head in compliance. Her eyelids felt heavy and she could feel the tiredness behind them. It dawned on her she had not slept since yesterday and so she rubbed her eyes and patted her face to wake herself up. She needed to stay alert.

The viewing process began and, for what seemed like an eternity, Ophidian after Ophidian entered the cave and examined Sheysu like a prize bull. None asked any questions, but many sniffed around her and touched her skin and her hair, then went to whisper into Dendro's ear. Sheysu shuddered repeatedly as leathery hands touched her, their faces so close she could feel their breath mingle with her own. She sensed Aurum's discomfort at the proceedings and Cain looked equally unhappy.

Dendro clapped his hands and said, "I think that is all the dignitaries for now. It has been a good day. Many of those men were my enemies, but now they have sworn their allegiance to me, just as I said they would. Sheysu, you have no idea of the power your presence has given me. I can see you are tired and in need of some refreshment." He sent his son out of the cave. A few moments later, he reappeared accompanied by a woman carrying a large tray of drinks. Her appearance was striking. She had the same scaly, blue skin common to many Ophidians. But it was her hair that made her stand out—a vivid, flame-red and copper colour which contrasted sharply with the blue of her skin. Like all Ophidians, her attire was scanty.

Dendro stood up for the first time and said, "This is my wife and our high priestess, Cenchrina."

Sheysu thought it odd that someone of such high status would serve drinks, but then she remembered the conversation about the poison. She looked at the tray and saw the cups upon it clearly divided into two groups. As Cenchrina walked around she handed Dendro and the other Ophidians drinks from one side of the tray. She then came to Sheysu and offered her a drink from the same side.

"Welcome, Sheysu. We have waited a long time for you to come." Sheysu recognised the voice from the hut. Cenchrina smiled at her, a sickly-sweet smile with no sincerity. Sheysu watched carefully and saw Cenchrina hand Aurum and the others drinks from the opposite side of the tray. The others looked over at Sheysu and she shook her head imperceptibly. The meaning was clear and the others held their cups without drinking them.

Dendro wasn't going to make it easy for them not to drink. His loud voice echoed out. "Let us drink to Sheysu and my new-found power." He raised his cup to his lips, but before he could drink, another group of Ophidians entered the cave.

"Chief Dendro." The first two Ophidians entering the cave spoke in unison. There were about ten Ophidians in all and the first two looked like brothers. They continued. "We have come to pledge our loyalty to you."

"Ah, the Cobra warriors. I am pleased you have finally seen the futility of your cause. Swear your allegiance to me and together we can lead Ophidia to rule over Animalia." Dendro's voice was triumphant. Sheysu looked at Cenchrina and her self-satisfied expression shared his victorious tones. The Cobra warriors had an air of defeat about them and their words were uttered through bitter lips.

A movement behind Dendro's throne caught Sheysu's eye. She strained hard to look, and as she gazed into the darkness, her heart leapt. Could it be? She kept looking. Yes, it was! Simione jumped high from the shadows onto the head of the stone Black Mamba that towered above the throne. She was carrying a large container, the contents of which she proceeded to pour over the heads of Dendro and those flanking him. Blue liquid spilled over their heads and faces. Dendro and the others screamed and clawed at their eyes as the blue paint, used for the skin shedding, burnt into their faces and eyes. Dendro dropped the black bag he had been carrying, and a Black Mamba wriggled free from its confines and slithered away. The Cobra warriors and their entourage, seeing this attack as an opportunity to regain their power, began to fight the other Ophidians in the cave.

Sheysu was overwhelmed with feelings of joy at seeing Simione, but had no time to express them as Simione jumped down and took her hand saying, "Sheysu, we must escape quickly while this commotion is going on."

Aurum, Lupinum, and Cain followed, dropping their poisonous drinks onto the floor. The Ophidians were too busy fighting each other to notice their departure. As they neared the entrance of the cave, Simione let out a shriek and fell over.

Sheysu, quick to her aid said, "What's wrong? What happened?"

Simione stood up and said, "It's nothing." She furiously rubbed her leg. "Quick let's get out of here."

Sheysu looked back before they left to see Dendro

flailing around, blindly hitting anything that came into his path. Once again she felt guilt and regret that her quest had caused so much damage and conflict. They emerged from the cave unseen and hid behind the statues before making their way furtively down the path leading to Dendro's home. The Ophidians in the arena were celebrating and feasting hard and were oblivious to their escape. The area around Dendro's home was deserted and they fled unnoticed into the jungle. They ran non-stop for as long as they could, without speaking, to make sure there was as much distance as possible between them and Ophidia.

They had been running for some time when, without warning, Simione collapsed. Sheysu, who had been behind her, was first to kneel by her side.

"Simione, what's wrong?"

But Simione did not answer. Her face was contorted with pain and dripping with sweat and her breathing was laboured. After a few seconds the painful spasm appeared to pass and Simione looked at Sheysu, her eyes heavy.

"I'm fine," said Simione, but her speech was slurred. Saliva began forming wet channels from the corners of her mouth. Her eyes slowly closed.

"Wake up, Simione. What's wrong?" The others had gathered around her now.

"Look at her leg," said Aurum.

Sheysu glanced down to see a red swelling on Simione's leg with dried blood at the centre.

"She's been bitten by something," said Lupinum, his voice grave.

"No! Not the Black Mamba from Dendro's bag!" exclaimed Sheysu. "Simione fell over at the edge of the cave. I didn't see anything, but what else could it have been?"

Simione opened her eyes.

"It's okay." Her voice sounded heavy as if she was drunk. "I've been bitten by snakes many times before, and I'm still here."

"We must go back and get the antidote," said Sheysu.

"NO!" Simione shouted, startling everyone. "I won't have anyone risking their lives for me. I'll be fine. We have to continue now we have the cure for you and your sister, otherwise what was the point of it all? We should be celebrating. Let me just rest for a while."

Tears welled up in Sheysu's eyes as she remembered Aurum's account of the soldier who died after being bitten by a Black Mamba. Surely there was no way to recover from a bite like this.

Sheysu looked over at Aurum helplessly.

"It would be a death sentence for anyone going back," said Aurum.

"But this is a death sentence for her. I can't let her die," replied Sheysu. "I'll go back. They won't kill me."

"Yes, but they won't let you leave, either, so what's the sense in that?"

Sheysu knew what he said was true, but she couldn't just sit there and watch Simione die.

"There must be something we can do."

Simione opened her eyes and spoke again. "I will be fine, Sheysu. It's okay. You don't need to worry about me. I've fought much worse than this and survived." She offered a weak smile. Her breathing was strained and her words were still slurred. "You must make the remedy for you and your sister from the Bushmaster. I will tell you how. You must take it as soon as possible. Its healing properties will travel through you to your sister in the same way her sickness passed through to you."

"Don't worry. Please rest, Simione," said Lupinum. "I have made remedies from snake venom many times before. I know what to do." Simione relaxed and closed her eyes once more. She was still sweating heavily and her breathing was shallow.

"Maybe the Bushmaster remedy could help Simione too," ventured Sheysu. "It must be worth a try."

"I don't know if it is similar enough, but it could be. I'll make the remedy now and we can try it," said Lupinum. He took the cage and asked everyone to give him their mugs, canteens and water.

Lupinum tore fabric strips from some bedding. He tied one section over the top of a mug and wrapped the remainder around one of his hands. Opening the Bushmaster's cage very carefully, he slowly put his covered hand in. The snake inside hissed. Lupinum tried to look in without putting his face too close. With one sudden movement he pulled the snake out, his hand clamped firmly around its neck. The snake squirmed wildly, trying to break free.

Its mouth was open wide and Lupinum pushed its upper jaw, fangs protruding, down onto the fabric cover of the mug. Its fangs pierced the fabric and after some time, Lupinum pulled the snake off and put it back into its cage.

"Did you manage to get enough venom?" asked Sheysu.

He pulled the fabric off the mug and let Sheysu look inside. She was amazed at how much venom there was. Lupinum poured water into the various mugs he had and then put a small amount of venom into the first mug and covered it with a plate and shook hard. Next he poured a small amount of the liquid from the first mug into the second one, which also contained water, and then shook again. Sheysu missed what he did next as Simione was restless again. She clutched her chest and her body arched in pain as she cried out.

"Hurry, Lupinum!" said Sheysu. "She's in so much pain."

"I'm nearly finished."

Lupinum poured some of the contents of the last mug into a canteen and gave the remainder to Sheysu.

"Here, give a sip to Simione, and you take a sip from the canteen."

Sheysu lifted Simione's head gently and put the mug to her lips. Simione opened her eyes, mustered up a strained smile and took a sip.

"I'll be fine, Sheysu," said Simione reassuringly.

Sheysu then took a sip of her remedy from the canteen. After a few minutes Simione appeared to relax. Her strained expression eased and her breathing became more regular.

"I think it's working," said Sheysu excitedly.

She stared intently at Simione, waiting for any signs of change, any small hint that recovery was on its way. The painful spasms stopped, whilst the saliva that had been dripping from her mouth dried up and her perspiration lessened.

Sheysu relaxed, confident the remedy was helping. She was so tied up with watching Simione she didn't notice the feeling of lightness surging through her own body after drinking the remedy.

Taking Simione's hand, she gently stroked it and just sat like this for some time, watching for signs of improvement. Her own tiredness took hold and her head repeatedly drooped and shot back up as she fought an overwhelming desire to sleep. Aurum touched her shoulder, causing her to jump.

"Sheysu, get some sleep. I'll keep watch over Simione."

But Sheysu shook her head. "No, I want to stay here." She was still holding Simione's hand when another painful spasm reared its head, causing Simione to tighten her grip and arch her back. She began trembling non-stop and droplets of perspiration rolled off her skin.

"It's stopped working. She's getting worse," said Sheysu, looking at Lupinum.

"It was doubtful it would help. We could try it again," replied Lupinum.

Sheysu shook the cup and then raised it again to Simione's mouth. Simione managed to take a sip between the painful tremors, but her eyes remain closed. They waited for a change, but this time, there was no respite. The spasms were getting closer and closer together.

Simione opened her eyes with effort. She raised her hand and touched Sheysu's face.

"Sheysu." Her voice was heavy and thick. "You are destined for great things. It is no accident you are here. This journey has been a harsh one...." She paused as her body contorted in pain. When it passed, she continued. "You can see how tribal hostilities have caused misery and death, even for a peaceful quest such as yours. As a mixed-blood you are rare, and even more unique in that you have Mineralian blood, and were raised in Planta. You cannot feel it yet, but you have the ability to unite the tribes and the kingdoms. Remember this after I am gone."

Sheysu gasped. "No, Simione! You cannot leave me. You cannot die. I should never have brought you." Tears bubbled from Sheysu's eyes.

"Let go of your guilt. I have no regrets. My job is done. I have helped you to live and I too will live on"—she touched Sheysu's forehead and chest—"in here and in here."

Another paroxysm of pain passed through her, stronger than the ones before. The spasms kept coming hard and fast and Simione struggled to breathe. Her body trembled violently for what seemed an eternity and then stopped abruptly, her limbs falling lifelessly. Very gently, Sheysu lifted Simione and hugged her close as she rocked back and forth, sobbing over her beloved, departed friend.

# REMEMBER ME?

The others let Sheysu sit with Simione undisturbed until she was ready to let go. Lupinum spoke first. "I will take Simione's body back to the Canidae village so her mother can bid her farewell. The quickest way back will be by river. Sheysu, Aurum, that is also the quickest way for you to get back too."

"If it's the quickest way, why didn't we come on the river?" asked Aurum, looking confused.

"We are upstream. The current would have been against us all the way and there are a few rapids to contend with as well. Going back, the current will speed us through and the rapids will be easier to navigate. We should get closer to the river and then build a raft to take us back. First of all though, we must make a makeshift stretcher to carry Simione."

"Yes, of course," said Sheysu, absentmindedly. "Simione's mother—how am I going to face her? Simione came to help me and now she is dead and I am alive! Was it worth it? So many deaths and bloodshed to save me and my sister." Sheysu felt empty. She had the cure she had been seeking, but it was a hollow victory.

Aurum came over to her. "I know this is hard,

Sheysu, but you cannot give up. Simione knew the risks. We all did. You can't hold yourself responsible for her death."

"How can you say that? If it were you, you would definitely be blaming yourself. Don't deny it."

"You're right. But then I would need somebody to tell me, as I'm telling you, not to give up. If Simione means so much to you, don't let her death be in vain. We've got to finish what we started. You've taken the remedy and it may help your sister, but the best way is to take it to her. Time is still of the essence."

Sheysu knew he was right, but the painful guilt in her soul would not be soothed. She would just have to carry it with her while she completed her quest.

Cain and Lupinum began making a stretcher while Aurum helped Sheysu to wrap Simione in some of the bedding. Together, they gently carried her and laid her onto the stretcher once it was complete.

"By my reckoning," said Lupinum, "the river is a couple of hours from here. We'll head towards it and make camp by the river's edge. Then we can build a raft and get some rest before the last leg of our journey."

They walked silently to the river, no one in the mood for talking. Sheysu had mixed feelings about journeying back by river after her earlier, near-death experience in its potent currents. But the feelings paled in insignificance against the trauma surrounding Simione's death. Surely nothing could be worse.

At the river's edge, Lupinum, Aurum and Cain began to build a raft, leaving Sheysu to set up camp.

She felt numb and went through the motions of organising the bits of bedding and food that were left.

In no time at all, the three men had built a fairly impressive raft. They pushed it close to the river's edge, ready to begin their journey home. Normally, she would have praised their efforts, but instead, she just looked at the raft fleetingly, seeing it only as bits of wood and vine.

Sheysu sat close to the fire she had made, but its warmth offered her no comfort.

"We have very little food left for the journey," said Lupinum. "Cain and I will quickly hunt for supplies and hopefully be back before nightfall. We can then set off at first light." With that, Lupinum and Cain disappeared into the jungle.

Aurum sat next to Sheysu by the fire. They stayed like this, silently, for what seemed like an eternity. The light faded as the sun lowered in the sky.

Lupinum and Cain had been gone for a long time when Sheysu heard shouting in the distance.

"Did you hear that?"

Aurum looked at her, his expression vacant, as if he had been miles away.

"No, I didn't hear anything."

"I could've sworn I heard someone shouting."

They both listened carefully for some time, but no further sounds were forthcoming.

"The jungle is full of all sorts of strange noises, but I'll go and take a look just to make sure," said Aurum.

"No one is going anywhere." A man stepped out

from the trees and pointed a gun at them. Sheysu recognised his voice. It was the stranger who had helped them to escape from the Arachnids. But this time she could see his face. It was puffy and dirt-ridden. He looked in need of a good wash.

"Mercurius, you low-life, I should've known it was you," said Aurum, looking at the man with disgust.

"You know him?" asked Sheysu.

"Yes, he's one of Queen Platina's shadier acquaintances."

Sheysu wondered why she felt no fear from the gun pointed at her, but then realised she was too numb to care.

"So what devious plan has Queen Platina hatched with you, Mercurius?" asked Aurum.

"Ah, Aurum the do-gooder. You can thank me later for saving you from the Arachnids, but then again, there'll be no need to."

"What do you mean?"

"Well, as you may know, helping Queen Platina has always served me well. Your uncle, the king, was my enemy and treated me unfairly at every turn. He had to go, and Queen Platina has since been a welcome ally, although I'm not sure for how much longer I can trust her. She asked me to follow you and bring back Similia, which is exactly what I am doing. Unfortunately, I cannot bring back the two of you. We cannot risk you becoming king, Aurum. I think you would be too much like your uncle, upright and honourable, and we can't have that. So I'm sorry, but I shall be taking Similia"—he picked up the Bushmaster's cage—"and heading back to Mineralia after killing the two of you. Any last requests?"

"So was it you that killed my uncle?" asked Aurum.

Mercurius was slow to answer, his expression distant, as if recalling a favourite memory. He then smiled with the satisfaction of someone who had accomplished a great deed. His smile revealed rows of rotting teeth and Sheysu shuddered with revulsion.

"The king made it so easy. I still remember the look of shock on his face. Knives have always been my weapon of choice, but it was my first murder using a straight razor. I think they are sometimes referred to as cut-throat razors. A very apt name, don't you think?"

"The king should've gotten rid of you when he had the chance. You'll pay for your treachery. I'll make sure of that."

"That may be a bit difficult from your grave."

"You can't kill us. We haven't found Similia yet," said Sheysu, stalling for time.

"Don't lie. I know Similia changes form, otherwise why would you have risked so much to battle the Ophidians?"

"You're mistaken. It's not Similia. We never found him, but we did find the cure for my sister while searching for him and it's the venom from that snake."

"I don't believe you. Anyway, even if it is the cure, then it will be just what Queen Platina needs."

"You don't understand, do you? The cure is different for every person. The same remedy won't work on everyone. Why else would I have come so far in search of it?"

Mercurius shifted restlessly on his feet, looking suspicious but confused.

"What do you think Queen Platina is going to do," Aurum broke the silence, "when you come back without Similia and give her a cure that doesn't work? I don't think you'll have your powerful ally anymore. Do you?"

"Lies, all lies. Why should I trust you? You have nothing to lose and everything to gain." His words were spoken with conviction, but yet a thread of doubt remained in his voice.

Sheysu wondered what was taking Lupinum and Cain so long, and then remembered the shouting she had heard.

"What was that shouting I heard before you came?" asked Sheysu.

"Oh, that was your two friends trying to escape from me before I dealt with them."

"What do you mean dealt with them?" Sheysu looked horrified.

"Not that it's any of your concern, but I haven't killed them yet. They are tied up. I lost my knife in the explosion at the Arachnid village, and shooting them would've made too much noise. But don't worry. I'll finish them off on my way back. Speaking of which, I have wasted too much time on you already. Whether this is Similia or not, I'll have to take my chances. But one thing is certain. I cannot let you live."

Mercurius walked towards them, aiming his gun at Aurum's head.

"Let Sheysu go. She can't harm you or Mineralia. You have no quarrel with her." Aurum looked at Mercurius beseechingly.

"A noble request, Aurum, and no less than I would expect from you, but it is something I cannot do. I never leave a prospective enemy behind. I have too many of those already."

*"Sheysu, can you hear me, are you still alive? Please answer me!"* Sheysu looked around searching for the source of the desperate voice, but saw no one. The voice sounded close by, but then she realized it was Cain speaking to her in her thoughts.

*"Yes I am. Where are you?"* Sheysu asked silently.

*"I'm on my way. Lupinum is unconscious."*

*"Please hurry. I don't think we have much time."*

Sheysu watched helplessly as Mercurius pushed his gun against Aurum's head.

"Wait!" cried Sheysu. "I can help you find Similia. Simione told me how before she died. We just need to travel a little farther." Sheysu lied, hoping to delay Mercurius long enough for Cain to get there.

Mercurius eased his gun away from Aurum's head and looked at Sheysu, one eyebrow raised sceptically. "This better not be a delay tactic, otherwise, I will take pleasure in killing you first!"

"No, no, I swear it's true. Simione said if we had stayed at the Valley of Sensation longer, Similia would have come. His energy was definitely guiding me, so maybe his physical presence just hadn't reached the valley yet. Simione was right about everything. I know it's the truth." Sheysu embellished her lie to make it sound plausible. It was working. Mercurius hesitated as if wrestling with an internal dilemma. While he was preoccupied, Sheysu caught a flash of movement in the trees behind him. The next second, Cain hurled himself at Mercurius, knocking him over and then held him from behind whilst trying to grab his gun. Aurum leapt onto the fighting pair and the three rolled around, flailing and kicking. Mercurius was a force to be reckoned with, managing to resist both Aurum's and Cain's efforts to overpower him. Suddenly, a single gunshot halted the struggle and Sheysu's heart stopped as she envisaged her worst fear. Had Aurum been killed? The sun's last rays of light faded from the sky and she strained hard to see what was happening with only the flickering flames from the fire to light the fighting trio. Cain dragged himself from under Mercurius and slowly stood up. He was holding Mercurius's gun and there was blood on his shoulder. But Mercurius was still alive and trying to escape the confines of Aurum's arms, which were now gripped tightly around his chest. His strength appeared to be flagging as he grimaced in pain. Sheysu breathed a sigh of relief on seeing that Aurum was not dead.

Cain pointed the gun at Mercurius and said, "You can let go, Aurum."

Aurum let go reluctantly. "I wouldn't do anything foolish, Mercurius. Cain won't hesitate to kill you."

Mercurius said nothing and just lay limply on the floor, his previous energy having deserted him. Sheysu moved closer and could now see a dark stain spreading across the black fabric on Mercurius's chest.

Sheysu looked at Cain. "What happened to your shoulder?"

"During the struggle, I held him from behind and managed to grab his gun. Somehow it fired and the bullet travelled back through him and ended up in my shoulder." Cain winced as he finished talking.

"We don't have any time to lose," said Aurum, rising to his feet while dusting himself off. "For all we know, Mercurius could have accomplices nearby. I wouldn't trust anything he says. We have to leave on the raft as quickly as possible."

"What are you going to do with Mercurius?" asked Sheysu. "I don't want any more bloodshed."

Aurum looked at the would-be assassin. "Then we'll just have to tie him up and leave him here. But that's as good as a death sentence for him. He won't survive for long with an open wound in a jungle full of wild animals."

"Well then, let's not tie him up. For all his failings, he did save our lives. Give him a fighting chance at least. There is no way he can catch us on foot if we're on a raft," said Sheysu.

"Ok, if that's really what you want. But I'm going to tie him up until we're ready to leave."

Sheysu nodded in agreement and then turned to Cain. "Let me look at your wound."

"I'll manage. I must go and find Lupinum." Cain handed Aurum the gun and then headed back in the direction he had come from. Sheysu was surprised and almost impressed at Cain's loyalty to Lupinum.

"Take me with you." Mercurius's pain-filled

voice came weakly from the floor. "I promise I will not harm you in any way. Just don't leave me to die in this Godforsaken place. You have my word."

"Nice try, Mercurius," said Aurum. "Sheysu might fall for your games, but not me. I'm sure you've been in stickier situations than this. You'll do just fine. I have no doubt someone as slippery as you will be able to trick even the wildest of animals and then easily find your way back to Mineralia."

"Sheysu, keep this gun pointed at Mercurius while I tie him up." She took the gun from Aurum and held it half-heartedly while aiming it at Mercurius. Aurum pulled some vines off a nearby tree and proceeded to drag a moaning Mercurius into a semi-upright position against another tree whilst tying him up tightly with the rough vines.

"You need me, Aurum," Mercurius spoke weakly. "Remember, if it weren't for me, none of you would still be alive. Mineralia will not be the same place you left behind. Before I left Mineralia, Queen Platina confided in me that she was planning to impose a curfew and kill all those who speak out against her. It won't be easy for you to go back and take the throne. Everyone lives in fear of the queen and allies will be thin on the ground. I could help you. The queen still trusts me and I can get close to her without a problem. I could make her demise quick and simple. If I don't come back with Similia, then as you say, I will have lost her allegiance, so I've got nothing to lose. I'm a good ally to have, Aurum. Being a king—even a righteous one—still means there are unsavoury tasks that have to be performed. You need someone like me."

"You may well be right, Mercurius. But your methods will not be my way. How could I ever trust you? How long before you switch your allegiance to another, and I find myself staring at your knife?"

"No, I swear. I will follow you for life!"

Aurum laughed. "Desperate men say desperate things. Relax, Mercurius. Thanks to Sheysu, today is not your day to die. I have no doubt you'll find your way back to Mineralia and that we will meet again, as adversaries, I suspect."

Mercurius slumped in defeat within the confines of the vines entrapping him, realising Aurum could not be swayed.

Cain reappeared from the undergrowth, but was now, surprisingly, being supported by Lupinum.

"Lupinum, thank God you're okay. What happened?" asked Sheysu.

Lupinum looked around, his eyes settling on Mercurius. "That reprobate knocked me out cold. I didn't see or sense him coming, which is rare for me. I came round when Cain found me, but now he's not doing so well. He's losing blood. We have to try and patch him up and get him back home."

"Here, let me take a look," said Sheysu.

Lupinum gently lowered Cain to the ground. "I'm going to get the raft ready. We really need to set off as quickly as possible."

"I'll help you," said Aurum. "Sheysu, don't worry about Mercurius. He's tied up tightly so he's not going anywhere." Aurum and Lupinum walked off towards the raft.

Sheysu knelt down beside Cain.

"How are you feeling?" she asked.

Blood was oozing out of the wound in his shoulder and down his arm. She reached over for the last bits of bedding nearby and tore them up into strips. She placed one of the strips over the wound and held it in place with firm pressure.

"I just feel weak. It's all gone wrong. There's no point in saving me."

"What do you mean?"

"Look at me, Sheysu. My life is worthless. I'm nothing but the general dogsbody for the tribe. Who could ever love me knowing that? How pathetic is my life that I even have to resort to blackmail to get a wife? I wouldn't blame you, Sheysu, but do you really hate me?"

"I think hate is too strong a word."

"When you saved me from the Ophidians, I couldn't believe it. I don't think I would've done the same thing if I'd been in your position. That changed everything for me. I began to believe that maybe you had started to care about me and I felt something I had never experienced before, love, hope—call it what you will. My life started to have meaning. All I know is that I loved that feeling and wished it could be true. Suddenly, all the hate I felt towards your family seemed distant and small. All I could think about was you, Sheysu, and how it would feel if you married me because you wanted to. Do you remember when I took you after running from the

Leonines? We had a connection. You can't deny it. You felt something for me."

Sheysu shifted around awkwardly, unable to look at Cain while he was speaking.

"That's when it hit me. I couldn't force you to marry me. I don't want to hold you to our deal. Maybe your feelings towards me have changed. Have they? Do you think you could marry me willingly?"

Cain looked up expectantly. Sheysu was at a loss for words. Was he deluded? How could he ever imagine she would marry him freely? Did he really mean it when he said he wouldn't hold her to his horrendous deal or was he just trying to trick her? She had to tread carefully. He had a quick temper—that much she knew. She couldn't risk enraging him and thereby causing a quicker death sentence for Aurum. Lying was her only real option.

"I really don't know, Cain. What you are asking for is not impossible. Maybe my feelings will grow over time. But for now, we really need to concentrate on getting back to the Canidae village and getting you fixed up."

"Don't listen to her. She's lying!" shouted Mercurius. Sheysu looked up startled, having forgotten he was there.

"Keep your lying mouth shut!" shouted Cain.

"You're angry because you know I speak the truth." Mercurius would not be quieted. "I don't know the situation between you, but trust me, I know people. Your story is plain to see, and at this moment, she will say and do anything to protect that which is at risk."

Cain looked at Sheysu seeking reassurance.

"Don't listen to him. He doesn't know me or you, and it serves his purpose to drive a wedge between us all, in the hopes someone will free him."

Cain seemed satisfied with her answer.

The bleeding from Cain's wound was subsiding and Sheysu tied a makeshift bandage, with the strips of fabric she had torn around his shoulder and chest. Just as she was finishing off, Aurum and Lupinum walked back.

"Let's pack up and go. The raft is ready," said Aurum.

Sheysu looked over at the raft gently bobbing at the river's edge and couldn't quite believe they were actually going home.

Aurum untied Mercurius, leaving one vine tightly knotted around him.

"That should take you a while to undo, and will give us the time we need to gain a head start on the river," said Aurum.

"If you leave me here, I won't forget this. I hope you can all sleep well in your beds at night because mark my words, during one of them, I will find each and every one of you and kill you!" Mercurius shouted his chilling threat at all of them as they walked towards the raft.

"Are you sure you want to leave him alive?" Aurum asked Sheysu.

"Yes. He's angry now, but when he gets back to Mineralia, he'll have more important matters to deal with, not the least of which will be pacifying Queen

Platina, and this day will become a distant memory. I don't believe he will have the time or the effort to carry out his threat."

Lupinum helped Cain onto the raft, then gently lifted Simione's stretcher with Aurum's help and placed it centrally on their return vessel. Sheysu turned around to take one last look at the harsh jungle landscape that had been home to such horrendous violence and the untimely death of her cherished companion. She sighed, relieved that the most difficult part of their journey was over, but then stole a glance at Cain and wondered if the worst was yet to come.

# THE JOURNEY BACK

Sheysu stared at the water foaming against the sides of the raft as it cut through the river, journeying ever closer to the Canidae village. They had been travelling for some hours and the dawn sun lifted the darkness with its warm light. Lupinum and Aurum took turns between steering the raft with the rudimentary rudder they had made and paddling at the side with the large wooden oar they had fashioned out of a cut branch. Cain lay in a semi-erect position and moaned periodically from the pain of his gunshot wound. Space was tight and Sheysu found herself wedged between Cain and Simione's stretchered body. Cain seemed determined to continue their earlier discussion and whispered to Sheysu.

"Have you thought any more about what I said?"

Sheysu lowered her head so she was close to Cain's ear and whispered, "Cain, this isn't the time or place to talk about it."

"I have to know. We will soon be back at my village, and then you'll be leaving to go back to Planta. You must decide now. I've already said I won't hold you to our agreement, so you are free to choose knowing I won't harm Aurum."

"Who won't harm me?" said Aurum, his words cutting loudly through the cloak of whispers they had woven around them.

Sheysu's head shot up, startled, and Cain moaned loudly in pain as the shock of Aurum's words caused him to jump involuntarily.

"You.... you, must've misheard." Sheysu stumbled over her words as she desperately searched for a plausible reason.

"I know what I heard, Sheysu. This just confirms my suspicions. Something strange has been going on between the two of you ever since we left the Leonine territory and it's not the new love you say you've found!"

"Tell him, Sheysu," said Cain. "Tell him how you are going to marry me!"

"That, I already know, but what has that got to do with harming me?" asked Aurum.

"It's not important now. Just leave it, Aurum," said Sheysu.

"No. I want answers and I want them now. This conspiracy, or whatever you call it, has been going on for too long!"

"Yes, I too would like to know what this is all about." Lupinum's voice came from behind as he steered the rudder.

Cain looked at Sheysu and shook his head with a look forbidding her to tell anyone. She knew if Lupinum found out about Cain's treacherous plan, his life back at the Canidae village would become untenable, and that was supposing Aurum would even let him live once he knew the truth. Cain had said his threat to Aurum no longer stood, but would he honour that if she told the others the truth? She owed Cain nothing, but somehow, even after everything he had put her through, Sheysu knew she would feel guilty if her actions resulted in his punishment or death. Still, she had no other option but to tell the truth as no acceptable lie was forthcoming.

She raised her head to look at Cain, and as their eyes met, his expression changed to one of fear, as he realized what she was about to do. Before she could utter her first word, Cain jumped up, rocking the raft in the process, and dove headfirst over the side. Water sprayed from the river covering them in fine droplets. Initially, stunned silence followed his dramatic departure, but then Lupinum stood up ready to go after him.

Sheysu pulled him back. "Let him go, Lupinum. It is for the best."

"I don't understand. Cain's loyalty to me, to the tribe, has never wavered."

They watched the water, their eyes following its rolling ripples for signs of Cain, but there was nothing. The river continued its journey as before, and revealed no clues as to his whereabouts.

Sheysu could not believe Cain had disappeared. Was he dead? Lupinum answered her silent thoughts.

"Cain is a very good swimmer. He would not drown, although his injury may hamper him. So tell me, why is it best for me not to go after my tribesman?"

"I'm not sure where to begin," replied Sheysu, hesitantly. "I think it really started when we were separated after running from the Leonines, although Cain's behaviour before that had also concerned me."

Sheysu continued her account of Cain's blackmail deal; their combined Canidae history, Aurum's involvement and Cain's subsequent recent retraction of his threat.

While telling her story, she occasionally looked over at Aurum, who remained quiet, to see his expression change from one of incredulity to one of anger. When she had finished speaking, it was as if Aurum could contain himself no longer.

"You should've told me, Sheysu. You had no right to keep this from me. It is my duty to keep you safe, not the other way round!" Aurum almost shouted the words.

"What was I supposed to do, let him kill you?" Sheysu was hurt that he was angry with her. Did he not understand she had been willing to sacrifice her future to save him?

"Do you really think I couldn't have defended myself against Cain?"

"If you knew the attack was coming, then yes. But what if he caught you unawares?"

Aurum appeared to calm down.

"So everything you said about having feelings for him was a lie?" asked Aurum, his turquoise eyes searching her face for clues.

Sheysu hesitated as the memory of her and Cain together in the tall bamboo flashed through her mind.

No, she didn't have feelings for him, but there was some kind of primeval attraction that made her shudder with revulsion as she remembered it.

"Yes, I had to say those things to keep my agreement with Cain."

"I cannot believe he was intending to challenge my right to be chief," said Lupinum, interrupting Aurum's line of questioning. "I never saw it coming," continued Lupinum, almost to himself. "I didn't realize he was so bitter. The events around his father's fall from grace are common knowledge amongst the tribe, but Cain never let it be known it affected him so deeply. It will be difficult for him to come back and live in the village now, after what will effectively be seen as his desertion. I don't know what he will do, although he is very capable of surviving in the jungle. There are a few exiled tribe members who have formed a small group of sorts and he may approach them."

*Cain must hate me even more now,* thought Sheysu. He had many reasons before, but now to be exiled from his home—surely that must top the list?

Aurum seemed keen to continue his questioning and jumped in before Lupinum could say anything else. "So let me get this straight. You have no feelings for Cain and have no intention of marrying him?"

"No, like I said before, I had to say those things. It was all a lie." Sheysu hated that she had lied to Aurum and his look of hurt and disappointment was more than she could bear. "I don't want to talk about this anymore right now. I just want to get back to the

Canidae village and give my respects to Simione's mother."

"Fine, if that's what you want," said Aurum, his expression a mixture of anger and disappointment.

Lupinum rummaged through the remaining rucksack. "We have very little food, barely enough for one meal, and we still have a couple of days on the river. I will need to stop and hunt, since our previous hunting trip was so dramatically interrupted. Let's keep going for a few hours to make sure there is no threat of Mercurius catching up with us, and then we can stop."

Sheysu scanned the banks of the river, looking for any signs of Cain. As much as she was relieved she was no longer subject to his threats, her guilty conscience weighed heavily and the pressure of one more death was more than she could handle. He was nowhere to be seen, and as they travelled farther along the river, she looked down to find her hands clenched anxiously into fists. With a loud sigh, she decided to give up her search for Cain and forced her hands to uncurl and relax.

Sheysu woke with a start, momentarily disorientated as the raft bumped into the riverbank. She didn't know how long she had been asleep, but the sun was now high in the sky, so at least a couple of hours. Lupinum jumped off the raft and tied it to a nearby tree.

"I will try and get some food for the rest of our journey. Aurum, it is best if you stay with Sheysu. Hopefully, there will be no unpleasant surprises this time."

Aurum nodded his agreement, and Lupinum ran off into the trees.

"Let's get into the shade," said Aurum as he stepped off the raft and headed inland. Sheysu followed, almost stumbling with drowsiness. They sat in the welcome shade, and within a few moments, she was asleep again.

Sheysu stirred and moaned in her sleep as she felt something press her face. She flicked her hand up to brush it away, but instead the pressure increased painfully and she flung her eyes open to find a hand clasped over her mouth. Looking up in panic, she saw Cain dripping with water, staring at her and urging her to be quiet with his finger in front of his lips.

"Shhh," he whispered. "Come quickly. We can take the raft and be back at the Canidae village before the others. I can still have my chance at being chief and we can still get married."

Sheysu looked at him with disbelief, but then saw him grab his knife and glanced over at Aurum who was sleeping peacefully. Such an easy target—it would take no effort for Cain to kill him. She had to do as he said. As quietly as she could, she rose from the ground, a sick feeling of dread worming its way through her. Cain grabbed her hand and led her roughly towards the river. Sheysu clambered onto the raft, while Cain untied the vine that secured it to a tree. She looked back to see Aurum one last time, but he wasn't there. Instead, he came running into her peripheral vision and threw himself at Cain, knocking him off balance.

"You don't know how long I've wanted to do this!" shouted Aurum as his fist landed hard against Cain's cheek. Cain, quick to react, swerved to avoid Aurum's next blow.

"Likewise," retorted Cain as he lunged towards Aurum with his knife, but Aurum managed to grab his wrist and twisted it until the knife fell from his hands. Cain's foot scuffed the floor, attempting to reclaim the lethal blade, but Aurum swung Cain around and kicked the knife far into the bushes. The strain of fighting took its toll on Cain's gunshot wound and a bright red stain began spreading through the wet bandage covering his shoulder. Their fighting styles were very different; Aurum was systematic in his movements, thinking ahead and intercepting each strike with ease, whilst Cain on the other hand, fought like a trapped animal, pouncing and attacking with savagery. Eventually, Cain showed signs of weakening and Aurum pinned him to the ground. He retrieved his gun from his belt and aimed it at Cain's head.

"No!" Sheysu's scream pierced the air. "Please, Aurum, don't kill him."

"He deserves to die, Sheysu. He's made your life hell!"

"I know…. I know. But let him be judged by the Canidae people. Let's tie him up and take him back to his village."

Cain grabbed Aurum's gun-holding hand and pushed the gun against his head.

"No…. Kill me now. My life there was a living hell. What do you think it's going to be after they find out what I've done? "

Aurum pulled his hand out of Cain's.

"Sheysu's right. You should be judged by your own people. You may have been given a lousy start in life, but you didn't have to do this. This was your choice and it shows what kind of person you are. You deserve everything you get."

"It's so easy for you to judge. Look at you—heir to the throne, a royal life since birth. The only direction in your life has been up. If you could imagine being at the bottom of the pile, knowing that's where you'll stay forever, then and only then could you even begin to understand what my life is like."

"I'm not you, Cain, so I can't pretend to understand what you've been through. But I still believe there is a better path than the one you've chosen."

"Aurum, he's bleeding heavily again. Let me tend to his wound and Lupinum can decide what's best when he returns."

Aurum nodded. "Don't try and escape, Cain. I'll still shoot you if I have to."

Sheysu knelt beside Cain and helped him to turn over as Aurum released his hold. As before, she applied pressure on the wound for some time until the bleeding stopped.

"How did you catch up with us?" asked Sheysu.

"It wasn't easy. I stayed under water for some time and swam behind some tall reeds, so you couldn't see me. There was a large piece of driftwood, which I managed to float on and used my hands to push it forward. Thankfully, the current helped me most of the way. I nearly missed you, but just caught sight of your raft as I was passing." Cain looked as if he wanted to say more, but Aurum was still standing nearby, watching him.

A rustling in the nearby trees made them all turn around. Lupinum walked towards them holding what looked like a small deer slung over his shoulder and a large handful of thickly rooted plants. He stopped mid-stride as he saw Cain lying on the ground.

"Cain, you have some nerve coming back!" exclaimed Lupinum.

Aurum stepped forward. "He came back to take Sheysu so he could carry on with his treacherous plan."

Lupinum continued, incensed. "How did you ever think you, of all people, could challenge my father and me to become chief? Your father has had to live with enough humiliation in his life. What do you think this is going to do to him—his only son a deserter and traitor?"

Cain said nothing, his expression unrelenting.

"What will happen to him?" asked Sheysu.

"The Elders will decide his fate. Being an Omega already, there are not many options left. He may be banished from the tribe."

Sheysu winced, another life ruined by her quest.

"Let's not waste any time. I will get this food ready and then we'll set off," said Lupinum, as he began to skin the small deer he had caught.

Aurum gathered some vine and tied Cain up, while Sheysu made a fire using Aurum's crystals and liquid.

With the food cooked and full stomachs, they set off on the raft again for the last leg of their journey back to the Canidae village.

# BACK AT THE VILLAGE

Sheysu's heart sank when the first tents of the Canidae village came into view. She'd had two days on the raft to think about what she was going to say to Simione's mother and she was still unsure. No mother should ever have to deal with the news she was about to impart. They left Cain tied up against a tree in the central clearing, where many Canidae women stopped what they were doing to stare at them.

"Lupinum, please, could you take me to see Simione's mother?" asked Sheysu.

"Of course, we'll all go."

They walked through the village, Aurum pulling the stretcher behind him, to a group of tents hidden by the jungle. Lupinum gestured towards one in particular and as they approached it, the canopy flung open.

Sheysu gasped with disbelief as there, stepping out of the tent, was Simione.

But how could it be?

Simione walked towards her, her mouth widening into a familiar grin. She came over to Sheysu and took her hands saying, "You must be Sheysu. I am so sorry I wasn't able to come and help you when you sent word for me. I myself was sick and it took quite some time for me to recover. Only two days ago did I start feeling better, and I have only just arrived, to see if there was anything I could still do."

Lost for words, Sheysu looked at the others, who both had the same incredulous expression on their faces. Then, at the same moment, as if their heads were all tied together they turned to look at the stretcher. Aurum lifted the bedding. It was empty.

She kept staring at Simione, her thoughts bouncing around chaotically, when a realisation hit her, and she said one word that explained it all. "Similia."

Sheysu started laughing and Simione looked at her, confused.

She laughed hard from the irony of their search for Similia together with the overwhelming relief and joy that Simione was alive. Still laughing, Sheysu said to the group, "Can you believe it? We spent all that time looking for Similia and *she* was with us from the very start. Similia changes form—I've heard it so many times, but it never occurred to me that he would take on someone else's identity or that he would be a woman."

"I'm sorry. I don't understand what's going on," said Simione looking perturbed.

Lupinum spoke up. "A few weeks ago, I sent my tribesman to get your help. The next morning you showed up and then led us on a journey to the Valley of Sensation."

"But that's not possible. Yes, your tribesman came to see me, but I was too ill to travel. I had been bitten by a poisonous snake the day before." She pointed at her leg, and Sheysu looked in amazement, as there in exactly the same spot where the other Simione had been bitten, was a large scar.

"You see," continued Simione, "I was extremely ill, and for the next few weeks, I struggled to overcome the effects of the bite. I was delirious for much of the time and slipped in and out of consciousness. The strange thing is that I had extremely vivid dreams, and when I just saw you now, Sheysu, it was as if I already knew you, all of you in fact. I can't explain how, but I feel we have been close."

"Do you remember any of your dreams?" asked Sheysu.

"Yes, but they were extremely bizarre—fighting with a huge Arachnid and large blue Ophidians—to name but a few."

"You won't believe this, but your dreams actually happened. Somehow Similia took on your form and then led us to the Valley of Sensation. We had some violent encounters with the Arachnids and Ophidians and a close escape from the Leonines."

"I've never heard of this Valley of Sensation. What is it?" asked Simione.

"The other you, or Similia should I say, took us there saying it was a place to connect with Similia's energy and help find the cure. It's the most beautiful place I've ever been to."

"I wish I could have gone there," said a wistful Simione.

Sheysu squeezed her hands. "I'm just so glad that you are here with us now."

"So what are your plans now? Do you have the cure you were seeking for your sister?"

"Yes. I need to go back to Planta to give it to her, but Similia said it would already be working through me. It seems strange to go home now. So much has happened, and I don't know how to say goodbye to you. I will miss you all so much—strange as that must sound, Simione."

"No, I feel it too. Our connection is deep and not yet finished, I suspect."

Lupinum stepped forward. "Sheysu, will you come back to Animalia? You will always have a home with the Canidae. If you do decide to come back, light two fires at the entrance of Animalia and we will find you."

"Thank you, Lupinum. I really don't know— maybe someday I'll come back. Part of me would love to experience my heritage, but I have to get back to my family and"—Sheysu looked longingly at Aurum— "there is nothing else to keep me here." Lupinum must have sensed there was more to be said and tactfully asked Simione to help him with Cain, and the two left Sheysu and Aurum alone.

Sheysu looked up at Aurum, her heart racing as it always did when their eyes met. But the warmth she had seen in his eyes before was not there. The memory of when he discovered she had been lying to him flashed through her mind, and she ached with the regret of knowing she had ruined their chances of being together.

"I'm sorry, Aurum. I'm sorry I lied. But you have to believe I only did it to protect you." Her voice choked with sobs as she continued. "I know you have a life all set up for you back in Mineralia, and our paths may never cross again, but I hope that one day you'll be able to forgive me."

Aurum crossed the small distance between them and put his finger on her lips. "Ssshh," he said to quieten her sobs. His turquoise eyes looked deep into hers. "I love you, Sheysu. With the chaos of our worlds falling apart around us, being with you has given me hope and a feeling of togetherness that I have never known. How could I be angry with you? You, who have been willing to sacrifice your future to save mine."

Sheysu saw the warmth in his eyes once again and felt Aurum's hands cup her face as he leant towards her and tenderly kissed her lips. For those few moments, the ache in her heart was replaced by a joyous thrill and she kissed him back, almost desperately, never wanting this moment to pass.

After the kiss, Aurum held her close. She clung to him tightly, waiting for some cruel hand to shake her and wake her from this blissful dream. But the hand never came and Sheysu relaxed, finally believing that all of this was real.

"What will you do now?" asked Sheysu.

"Come with me. Help me to reclaim Mineralia. It won't be easy. But after everything we have come through together, I'm sure we will succeed. I cannot imagine living a day of my life now without seeing you."

Sheysu gasped. Was Aurum actually asking her to

be with him—to live in Mineralia? A seed of doubt remained.

"What about Argonisa?"

"Don't worry about her. It was a formal arrangement made many years ago. I have no doubt she will understand and give us her blessing. Her relatives may feel differently, but I'm sure we can pacify them somehow. Please say yes."

Sheysu gently brushed Aurum's golden hair from his face and let her hand rest against his cheek.

"Yes, of course my answer is yes. I love you, Aurum. I came to Animalia to find a cure, but with you, I have found my future."

They kissed once more and the pain of the past few weeks melted from her body.

"I have to go back to Planta first. Somehow it doesn't feel like home anymore. I hope they'll understand."

"I would love to come with you, but I fear things are changing rapidly in Mineralia and I must get back as soon as possible to prevent a catastrophe."

"I know you have to go. I have been so lucky to have you for so long. For all of Queen Platina's deviousness, I will be forever grateful to her for bringing us together."

"As always, you see the positive in others."

"I will go back to Planta first and then join you in Mineralia."

"Please come quickly. I don't know how long I can cope without seeing you."

Sheysu smiled knowing that nothing, in all of the kingdoms, could stop her racing back to Aurum.

# EPILOGUE

A different Sheysu approached the familiar landscape of Planta. Her quest had forever changed her in so many ways, that she could not even begin to comprehend the far-reaching effects it had had. As she approached the house she had lived in for as long as she could remember, she was struck by the thought, *This is not my home anymore.* A lump formed in her throat when she realized she was coming home to say goodbye.

The chickens in the front yard began squawking loudly, signalling her return. The front door flung open and her father took one look at Sheysu and turned to shout behind him, "Sheysu's back. Our beloved daughter has returned!"

Her mother pushed past him and ran down the steps to hug Sheysu, tears streaming down her face. Sheysu melted into the hug, allowing herself to be transported back to being a child lovingly held by the arms of her family as her father came to embrace them both.

They walked back to the house arm-in-arm, her parents full of questions about her journey. Her mother held her tightly as if she would never let her go. Once inside, they climbed the stairs to Kora's room. The door was open and as Sheysu walked in she was amazed to see Kora sitting up in bed, being propped up by a pillow."

"I knew you'd come back, Sheysu," said Kora. "I dreamt of you so often. After one particular dream I woke up from my long sleep, and I knew you had found the cure. I told Mama and Papa, and said you'd be home soon. Thank you for saving my life."

Sheysu rushed over to Kora and the two hugged each other tightly, their faces wet from tears of happiness that this nightmarish ordeal was finally over.

Wasting no time, Sheysu took the canteen Lupinum had filled with the cure, from her belt, and poured some of the precious liquid into the empty glass next to Kora.

"Drink this. It is what you have been waiting for and will complete your recovery."

As Kora finished drinking, her parents came to join them in a family embrace. Sheysu sat there, warm and nurtured, and wondered how she was going to tell them she could not stay. That tomorrow she would be leaving on another quest from which she might never return.

# ACKNOWLEDGEMENTS

Thank you to all my family and friends for your help and support. I am so grateful to have you in my life.

Special thanks to my beta readers (Aarti Patel, Charlotte Coates, Miriam Morris and Sasha Venchard) for their patience, wisdom, and encouragement. Thanks to all those who have read the book pre-publication. Your support is invaluable.

Special thanks also to Nino Khan for her fabulous cover.

To my brilliant editor, Amy Eye, thank you for your help and insights.

# A NOTE FROM THE AUTHOR:

Thank you for taking the time to join Sheysu on her journey. If you enjoyed this book and have a moment to spare, I would really appreciate a short review on Amazon.

The next book in the Sheysu's Gold Series will be called Reclaim. It will be available in 2015. If you would like to be sent information on the next book and notified of release dates, giveaways and pre-release specials then please sign up at:

www.sunitavenchard.com
www.facebook.com/SunitaVenchardAuthor

# ABOUT THE AUTHOR

Sunita Venchard lives in London with her husband and daughter. Her journey into writing books has been a long and serendipitous one, taking her through a myriad of roles; IT analyst and designer, homeopath, PC trainer and mother to name but a few. As a child she could be found reading the DC and Marvel comics discarded by her older brothers. From there she developed a passion for science fiction, fantasy, adventure and a love of books and films. Sunita felt almost compelled to write her first book and discovered that the process spirited her away into the realms of fantasy and adventure she had enjoyed as a child.